Vampires. Zombies. Wendigo. There are a million books about them, and of similar paranormal, undead creatures. Sparkly cutesy ones. Vicious evil ones. Heroic ones. Impossible to kill ones. Slow and fast ones. Some books even purport to tell you of their origins. Well, they're all bunk and bother, as Ob would say. Nothing but humbug.

This eighth volume of the Harbinger of Doom saga is different. It reveals the truth about those creatures. About where they really came from. About the terrible threat they posed and may still pose today. And about the brave folk of days long past that stopped them from overrunning the world.

BOOKS BY GLENN G. THATER

THE HARBINGER OF DOOM SAGA
GATEWAY TO NIFLEHEIM
THE FALLEN ANGLE
KNIGHT ETERNAL
DWELLERS OF THE DEEP
BLOOD, FIRE, AND THORN
GODS OF THE SWORD
THE SHAMBLING DEAD
MASTER OF THE DEAD
SHADOW OF DOOM
WIZARD'S TOLL
VOLUME 11+ (FORTHCOMING)

HARBINGER OF DOOM
(COMBINES *GATEWAY TO NIFLEHEIM* AND *THE FALLEN ANGLE* INTO A SINGLE VOLUME)

THE HERO AND THE FIEND
(A NOVELETTE SET IN THE HARBINGER OF DOOM UNIVERSE)

THE GATEWAY
(A NOVELLA LENGTH VERSION OF *GATEWAY TO NIFLEHEIM*)

THE DEMON KING OF BERGHER
(A SHORT STORY SET IN THE HARBINGER OF DOOM UNIVERSE)

To be notified about my new book releases and any special offers or discounts regarding my books, please join my mailing list here: http://eepurl.com/vwubH

GLENN G. THATER

MASTER
OF THE
DEAD

A TALE FROM THE
HARBINGER OF DOOM SAGA

Copyright © 2014 by Glenn G. Thater.

All rights reserved.

MASTER OF THE DEAD © 2014 by Glenn G. Thater

ISBN-13: 978-0692616543
ISBN-10: 0692616543

Visit Glenn G. Thater's website at
http://www.glenngthater.com

January 2016 Worldwide Print Edition
Published by Lomion Press

1

THE DEAD FENS, OUTSIDE THE KEEP

Year 1242, 4th Age
12th Year of King Tenzivel's Rule

Brother Donnelin bled from wounds at cheek, nose, arm, and hand; it hurt to breathe, ribs broken or badly bruised. He couldn't catch his breath. Karktan, Master Gorlick's lieutenant, was down on one knee, breathing heavily, battered worse than the priest, his face covered in blood, most of it his own. But they'd done their duty, those two soldiers. Before them sprawled the broken bodies of the half dozen Lugron warriors that dared charge their position at the keep's gate; down and out or dead were they, one and all.

After he'd felled the last of them, Donnelin saw a giant Lugron crushing Master Gorlick in a bearhug; the weapon master's body limp. The great man hung there, helpless, battle still raging about him. Donnelin couldn't believe his eyes. No one could beat that man, his grievous, infected arm notwithstanding — Gorlick the Bold, considered by many to be the greatest swordsman in all Lomion.

"**H**old here," Donnelin barked to Karktan as he sprang to Gorlick's aid, wheezing and coughing as he went. Karktan only complied because he hadn't seen what happened to his master. When Donnelin was halfway there, Gorlick went wild. He bit and tore at his attacker; his teeth his only remaining weapon. It was all the weapons master could do, his arms pinioned, no room to kick. Donnelin marveled at his tenacity, his fierce reputation well deserved.

Before Donnelin made it to Gorlick's side, the huge Lugron collapsed, Gorlick atop him. He tore at the Lugron's throat like a wild animal; blood spurted everywhere.

"Gorlick, roll off him; I'll finish him," spat Donnelin, his sword poised to action. He barely choked out the words, his breath gone from the effort of running there, his right side in agony.

Gorlick turned toward Donnelin as if to meet his gaze, but looked through him, his eyes wild, bestial; his expression, odd, vacant; his pallor, gray and sickly. Blood and gore dripped from his mouth. He licked his lips and swallowed.

He swallowed the blood.

Donnelin shuddered at the sight; his stomach twisted to knots even before his brain processed what his eyes saw. Something wasn't right; not right at all. "Master Gorlick," he said, though his words were barely a whisper. In the din of the battle, no one heard him.

Gorlick opened his mouth excessively wide, his lips curled back, exposing teeth, top and bottom; a long raspy inhale of breath.

Donnelin's eyes went wide; he sensed what was coming, prayed he was wrong. He quaked when he heard it. He wanted to clamp his palms to his ears and run screaming.

The croaking sound.

That's what he heard.

That's what roared from Gorlick's mouth.

A noise not meant to come from any living throat. The horrid sound of the things they named the shamblers. The eerie call of the living dead.

Donnelin froze.

His feet were rooted in place. He could not turn away. All he wanted to do was run.

To flee.

But he couldn't move. He couldn't think.

This can't be happening. It can't be.

The thing that once was Gorlick turned back toward the dying Lugron. It bit and tore at his throat, ripping off chunks of flesh, and devouring it, as the unholy, insatiable hunger took control.

The thing's gaze mercifully off him, Donnelin snapped out of his trance, though all color had fled from his face. He staggered backward a few steps and shook his head in disbelief before collapsing onto his backside. The impact took what breath remained in his lungs. His head spun, dizziness taking hold.

Lord Torbin Malvegil stepped up past Donnelin, his magnificent armor splattered with blood, his helmet gone, droplets of blood dripped from the end of his bare short sword.

"Gorlick!" cried Malvegil as he stepped forward, though he was not calling out to his friend, so much as mourning him, for he deduced at once what had happened. In that moment, he pieced it all together. He should have anticipated Gorlick's fate when they spied the shambling sailors that wandered through the Fen. He should have known that the bite on Gorlick's arm that festered so badly was no normal wound.

He'd been infected. Tainted. But whether by disease, poison, curse, or black magic, Malvegil had no idea, and at the moment, he'd didn't care. Only two things mattered: that the shamblers' bites were deadly, even the merest scratch, and that his friend, his beloved friend of long years, was dead and needed avenging.

Mayhap Malvegil saw this coming. Maybe he knew it as soon as Gorlick's wound began to fester. Maybe he just couldn't bear to face the truth of it.

The ghoul that had been Gorlick paid Malvegil's shout no heed and continued its bloody feast.

Malvegil's face grew dark. His expression morphed from shock and sadness to anger.

To rage.

He drew back his leg and kicked the ghoul with such force that it rose into the air and crashed down two feet away.

He wasn't kicking his friend, he told himself.

He kicked the thing that killed his friend.

Whatever unholy spark of life resided in that shambler had no place in Midgaard. Malvegil would destroy it. He would see his friend at rest. His soul at peace.

The ghoul rolled on impact and leaped up. Blood streamed from its mouth; death flared in its eyes; its agility, surprising; its movements, quick and sure. It came at Malvegil. It lunged at him. Snarling. Teeth gnashing. Murder in its eyes. It came fast.

Too fast for most men.

But not for the great lord of the Malvegils. He swung his blade but once; a precise cut; his skills honed over long years.

Gorlick's head flew from his shoulders. A clean cut, straight through the neck. That wound should have spouted blood, should have rained it all around like a crimson fountain.

But it didn't.

Barely any blood at all was there. For no heart pumped within Gorlick's breast. There was no denying the truth, if even the smallest doubt yet remained. Those things. Those things that wandered about the Dead Fens, croaking, gibbering, and hunting for flesh were no pitiful lepers. No deformed pariahs. No victims of some terrible, unknown wasting disease. They were not men, not people. They were not living, breathing beings at all. They were rotting corpses. Devoid of all life. Without spirit. Without any semblance of humanity. Without souls.

They were the dead. The shambling dead.

And whatever foul twist of fate made them thus was spreading, Gorlick only its latest victim.

As Malvegil began to turn away, Gorlick's headless corpse still stood — as such are sometimes wont to do when the blow is clean enough; the blade, sharp enough.

Malvegil waited.

Waited for the corpse to fall; to crumple to the ground as they always did after but a moment or two.

Seconds passed.

And still it stood.

Its undeath not yet extinguished. Not yet ready to give up the world of men.

Then the headless corpse did the unexpected.

It stepped forward.

One step and then a second.

It moved.

It walked.

Steady and strong went its advance, not stumbling, bumbling, or staggering. It moved with purpose. With intelligence.

Malvegil's mouth dropped open. He backpedalled. The thing reached for him, as if it could see him, hands turned to crimson claws.

He shrank from that embrace. He knew it meant a fate far worse than death. He fought to keep his nerve, not to panic, not to run, not to scream. Then Malvegil's face grew hard again; hatred in his eyes; vengeance in his soul. He lunged forward.

His thrust took the ghoul through the heart. He twisted the blade as he pulled it out. That strike would have instantly dropped any living man. Bled him out in seconds. But to the shambler, it was of no consequence.

Still it came on. Stepping forward yet again. And again no blood spurted from the wound.

From nearby, came a strange gurgling noise, once and then again. Then came the croaking sound of the dead. Not deafening as before, but strong, powerful, hungry, ravenous.

"The head," shouted Donnelin. "The head still lives."

Malvegil glanced over and saw with horror the severed head of Gorlick lolling on the ground, bloodshot eyes wide and darting, the mouth opening and closing, teeth snapping at the air: click, click, click, only a hair's breath from his ankle.

Malvegil jumped back, startled, nearly tripped over his own feet. A moment more and those jaws would have clamped down on his leg. If his armor had failed him, if he had suffered the merest scratch — his fate would've been sealed. He would have followed Gorlick unto death — undeath. Never to see Valhalla. Never to dine in Odin's hall with the gods; with his father, grandfather, and all the proud Malvegils that went before them; a storied line that stretched back beyond memory.

"Dead gods," cried Malvegil. "This cannot be. By all that's holy, this cannot be!"

Only blackest sorcery could be behind this. This curse. This horror. A fiend. A fiend from the pits of Helheim.

"Gods save us," said Donnelin. "The black arts."

Malvegil had to end this. Had to bring the creature down. He steeled himself against the horror. He put it from his mind. He concentrated on his anger. On his need for revenge. He maneuvered, evaded, swung his blade again.

He severed one of Gorlick's arms.

A second stroke took a leg.

Still the corpse advanced. It dragged itself across the cold ground. It moved unerringly toward Malvegil, as if even headless, it could see him, or sense him, but by what esoteric power Malvegil feared to fathom.

"It will not die," shouted Malvegil. He took its head, its arm, its leg. Still it came on.

Still its mouth croaked and gibbered, even detached from its lungs.

Still its jaws snapped in the air: click, click, click.

He could not stop it. He could not kill it. Dead gods! He grabbed Donnelin about the arm. They both backed away, their minds searching for some means to kill the thing.

Ob, that crusty old gnome, appeared, lit torch in one hand, wineskin in the other, blood dripping down his brow. He upturned the wineskin and doused the decapitated head. And doused the crawling corpse. And with the torch, set them both aflame.

The head roared, croaked, and wailed; its jaws still snapping: click, click, click. Its body thrashed about and pounded the ground, desperately trying to advance on the men.

But the flames were too much.

Indomitable will or no, its flesh was doomed. After a time, the fire did its work. The body and the head quieted; they stopped moving, as some final death took them.

Even as Ob, Malvegil, and Donnelin sighed in relief, the giant Lugron that had choked the life from Gorlick sat straight up, its throat torn out, head lolling to the side, nearly severed.

It croaked.

It gibbered.

It began to rise.

Ob flung the last of the wine over the Lugron shambler's head and jabbed it with the torch as it stood. The flaming ghoul flailed about, staggering to and fro, burning all the while. Some moments passed, moments that seemed like long minutes, before the thing finally collapsed and moved no more.

2

THE DEAD FENS, OUTSIDE THE KEEP

Year 1242, 4th Age
12th Year of King Tenzivel's Rule

As Malvegil, Ob, and Donnelin watched the giant Lugron burn, Lord Aradon Eotrus, Artol, McDuff the Mighty, and Par Talbon of Montrose approached the scene, each of them battered, bruised, and bleeding, the last of their opponents down and out or dead.

Then came more croaking noises from much farther afield. Malvegil looked toward the west. That's when he saw them. A glimmer of movement, hidden by distance and the mist. But he knew what was out there.

"The shamblers are coming," shouted Malvegil. "Move. Now. To the keep!" Malvegil nearly dragged Donnelin along. The priest couldn't take his eyes off of Gorlick's burning corpse. "It's dead," said Malvegil. "We've got to move or else we'll join it."

"It's Gorlick," said Donnelin, his voice raspy and strained.

"He's dead," said Malvegil. "Let's move."

It was hard for Malvegil to say those words, to believe, to accept, that his friend was dead. It all seemed a dream. Not real. That's what happened in battle sometimes. When things got bad. It didn't feel real.

Gorlick — a good man. Trusted. Loyal. Irreplaceable.

Malvegil had to accept that he was gone, but also, he had to put it from his mind. Not let it cloud or clog his thinking. There would be time enough to mourn when he was safely on the homeward road. Time enough to curse the gods for letting Gorlick become one of those things.

The Lomerians rushed for the keep's entryway. Karktan awaited them, still standing the guard. The portcullis was down. Several dead Lugron littered the passage beyond, visible between the thick steel bars.

The bars were reddish and uneven — their surfaces corroded, flaking, pitted, yet solid at their cores.

There was no bending them.

No breaking them.

Not with what they had on hand.

McDuff charged up to the gate, bent low, and tried to heave the gate up, his massive muscles bulging. "It's supposed to be open," he said, his accusing stare focused on Karktan.

The gate didn't budge.

"We tried—" said Karktan.

"Artol! Red Tybor!" shouted McDuff. "Step up here and put your backs to it. I can't lift this thing alone."

"Red Tybor is dead," said Ob, who looked half dead himself. Dirt and mud covered the top of his head. Blood smeared his face, dripped from his

15

nose, and streaked his tabard red. "And Gorlick too."

"Dammit!" cried McDuff as he looked over his shoulder to see who was left.

Malvegil spun around, his jaw now slack, disbelief covering his face. "The Pict?" he muttered. "The Pict is dead too?"

"Fought like a devil to the end, he did," said Ob.

Artol strained to lift the gate alongside McDuff, but the effort was still to no avail. They couldn't budge it.

Aradon and Karktan joined them. Ob got down on his hands and knees, ready to scurry under if they got it up high enough.

Aradon tried to get Malvegil's attention, to join them in lifting the gate. "Torbin," he said. "Torbin!" Malvegil paid him no heed, his gaze was fixed on the things that loped toward them out of the mist. Still a ways away were they, but drawing closer with each moment. There was no doubt that they were headed for the keep.

"Malvegil!" shouted McDuff. "Get your lordly butt over here and help with this gate."

Malvegil snapped out of his fugue and moved to aid them.

Par Talbon slumped on the ground beside the gate, holding his gut, unable to catch his breath.

The men pressed close together in order to get hold of the gate, too narrow for so many big men to easily grip at once. But all five were needed and then some. They grunted and struggled, but the gate held fast.

"They're getting closer," sputtered Donnelin as he stared out into the mist while holding his injured side. "They're moving slowly, but we've only got a minute or two." Donnelin pulled a holy symbol from his pack and held it out toward the shamblers, his hand shaking. "Dear gods, we're all going to end up like Master Gorlick," he said.

"It's stuck," said Ob. "Must have come down hard — the spikes at the bottom are dug solid into the cobbles. We've got to give it a heave, all together, at once. Once we get it moving, then it's just weight. We can lift it or prop it up. On three — one, two, three!"

Ob was right. With a concerted heave, the gate popped free, several cobblestones pulled up with it.

"Get something under it," said Aradon.

Ob and Donnelin shoved the remnants of the wagon under it, but the wood wasn't large or strong enough.

"Pull it higher so I can get under," said Ob. "I'll find the mechanism. There's got to be a winch inside."

The men rested the gate on the boards they'd shoved under it for a few moments, then heaved all together again.

"Six inches more," said Ob. "Just a wee bit more."

He went down on his belly and scurried through the moment the gate was high enough. Their strength spent, muscles trembling, the others dropped the gate as soon as Ob was clear.

The rotted wood shoring splintered with the impact.

"Find the winch and fast," said Aradon, breathing heavily as he leaned against the gate. "And Gabriel too if you can."

"Where is it? Where's the winch?" shouted Ob as he dashed in and out of the doorways on either side of the corridor, and waded through the brown water that quickly passed his knees. Farther down the corridor, it approached his waist, slowing his progress. "I don't see it."

"It's got to be there," said Aradon. "It must be hidden. Look for a panel on the wall. Some door that swings open."

"I have been. There's nothing."

Ob stepped around the corner. A moment later, they heard him curse. Then came a clash of arms — steel on steel.

"They're on him," said Artol. "More Lugron inside."

"They're almost here," shouted Donnelin as the group of loping, bedraggled figures emerged from the mist into clear view. "A hundred yards and closing."

"We're out of time," said Malvegil.

"If we freeze as before, will they see us?" said Artol.

"Too late for that," said McDuff. "They've already marked us and good. We either get through the gate now, make a stand here, or run for it. What say you, your lordships?"

"I'm too spent to run," said Aradon. "And I've no stomach for it anyways."

"I'll not run," said Malvegil. "If we can't get through, we make our stand here. But let's try the gate once more."

"Ob," roared Aradon as he took hold of the bars again. "Kill those buggers and find that damn winch! Get this thing opened now!"

Gasping and straining for all they were worth, the five warriors inched the gate up, but it stuck not six inches above the ground. Hopelessly jammed. It would go up no further. Nor would it come down.

"How many do you see?" said Malvegil.

"Thirty at least," said Artol. "Maybe forty. Maybe more farther back in the mist."

"Too many," said McDuff. "Ob, get the stinking gate up! Ob!"

"Keep lifting," said Par Talbon as he rose to his feet. He had bandages wrapped around his torso, just above the navel. Blood seeped through, though less than there could have been. Some Lugron's blade had sliced him up good. His face was pale; he looked ready to drop. "I'm going to try something," he said. "Be not alarmed and don't let go of the gate."

Talbon spoke olden words from the Magus Mysterious, that ancient language of the wizards. He stood behind the others, facing the portcullis, his hands upraised, palms forward. As he spoke the eldritch words, his hands began to glow, dimly at first, but then brighter, and then brighter still. Talbon's jaw was clenched; his face strained. Then the hands of the men lifting the gate began to glow as well. A power surged through their hands and their arms, one and all.

19

That power was something unseen but for the glow; something drawn from the magical weave, pulled through the ether, tapped by Talbon's mastery of magic. A power. A strength.

A sorcery.

Beyond the understanding of the common man was it. The depths and secrets of its nature beyond even the wizards' knowledge, though they were ever loath to admit as much. Talbon shaped the sorcery to do his bidding. He shaped it as skillfully as any but the most learned of the grandmasters of the Tower of the Arcane, at least with respect to war magic, for that was his specialty. He had stood at Lord Aradon's side in battle more times than he could remember. His magic and Aradon's might had held back the wild of the North for many years. That iron gate, however heavy, would not stop them.

And so he used his esoteric craft to make the men stronger. Stronger than any mortal ever was, albeit, but for a brief span. With the men's grunts and curses, the gate began to move up.

Even as it rose, the long line of shamblers picked up speed and headed straight for them. The noise spiked to a mind-numbing cacophony as they croaked and screeched at such a volume to threaten a man's hearing. To threaten a man's sanity. They ran headlong, screaming, as loud and as fast as any man ever could.

3

THE HOLLOW, FALSTAD MANOR

Year 801, 4th Age

"Penny!" screamed Lady Cassandra, her voice hysterical, her eyes wide and locked on her daughter's monstrous face as Pennebray loomed over her, carving knife in hand, murder in her eyes. Cassandra was tied fast down to the table: wrists, arms, shoulders, waist, and legs. She couldn't move at all. And until but a moment earlier, when Pennebray pulled the gag from her mouth, she couldn't speak.

"My baby!" she wailed, despair in her voice.

The raucous crowd, adorned in party masks and fine dress, shouted, "duchess," over and again, as Lady Dahlia looked on, triumph on her face, her sister's tiara newly placed upon her brow.

Azrael the Wise found himself leaping over the dining table at which he sat, sword in hand. No time to think. No time to figure out what was what. He'd ask questions later. First, he'd save Cassandra.

Pennebray placed the carving knife against her mother's throat.

"No, baby, please, no," cried Cassandra. "Snap out of it, baby. It's me. It's momma. I love you. Please. Help! Don't. Please!"

Azrael was halfway there when the creature that had been Pennebray pulled the knife across her mother's neck. She didn't do that in a rage. Nor did she do it coldly, devoid of emotion. She did it slowly, an evil leer, a slight grin, on her face. She savored the moment. She enjoyed it.

The blade cut deep.

A geyser of red blood shot towards the ceiling. Pennebray smiled as the spray washed over her face. Her unnaturally long tongue shot out and lapped it up from around her mouth and her cheeks.

A blur of motion took place around the room.

Folks were leaping over the tables.

Others were screaming.

Weapons came out.

Fangs were bared.

It wasn't just Pennebray that was a monster. They were all around Azrael. And they were out for blood.

Clawed hands grabbed at Azrael from this side and that, even as he ran. How fast they were to catch him. At least twice the speed of any normal person were they, those creatures, for Azrael was quick indeed.

Fangs.

Fangs where there should have been teeth.

Gray, sickly flesh.

Dead black eyes.

It seemed as if the whole of the crowd had instantly transformed into monsters of nightmare. Monsters like Penny.

Azrael slipped their grasp. He spun, sword working. Dagger too. Instinct in charge. Slicing flesh.

The screaming.

Blood, spurting.

Howls of pain.

They fell back from him, the monsters did. Shocked by his skill.

His weapons bloodied. The old fire in his eyes. His lungs pumping.

They shrank from his wrath. From his preternatural skill.

They cowered. Even in their numbers.

For Azrael was one of those that even monsters feared.

He killed.

And killed.

And killed again.

Around the room, those that wore the black party masks fell upon those that wore the red. The red were human — townsfolk. But not one amongst them was common. The invited were only the wealthiest, the most influential, and those known to be skilled at arms. They were the ones that could be a threat. A threat to the new order. A threat that was best eliminated in one fell swoop.

Those in the black masks were the monsters.

Fiends.

23

Fanged abominations were they: Penny, Lady Dahlia, Ebert Cook, Mikel Potter, the washerwoman, and many more.

Too many more.

Far more than those ten that Azrael treated with his serum. His instincts had been right all along. He was responsible for this horror, and all the horrors that had befallen The Hollow over the previous month. Though the truth it was far worse than he ever imagined.

The cure that he had labored for so long to find, was no cure at all.

It was a contagion. A disease.

A bloodlust.

And it was spreading.

A black mask, all fangs and claws came at Azrael, undeterred by the torn dead heaped about his feet.

Azrael was too quick. Too skilled. The clumsy creature, no match for him. He cut the thing to the bone, diagonally across the chest. A kick, a punch, and a shoulder knocked two other fiends back. For a moment, Azrael had space to breathe.

Dozens of black masks poured over the knot of red masks where sat the mayor, the constable and his men and their ladies.

Azrael couldn't get to them. The infected rolled over them like a wave. Surely, they perceived the lawmen to be their biggest threat. So they concentrated their attacks on them.

They ripped.

They tore.

They killed. Laughing as they went.

The people screamed. Innocent victims.

They begged.

Pleaded.

But no quarter was given.

No mercy was to be had.

Only taunts.

And death.

Terrible, violent death.

They had no chance. No chance to escape. No chance to survive.

The grand ballroom of House Falstad ran red with blood.

A wild melee it was. Some few red masks put up a fight, giving as good as they got. Swords were out. Daggers too. Someone had an axe.

Azrael hadn't been in such a battle in many years. But he hadn't forgotten. The old way of the sword was in his blood. As much a part of him as was breathing. His skills, still honed, practiced daily with his guardsmen, and in private.

He stayed ready. Vigilant. Prepared for those times when his skills were needed. Though he never let his men see the depth and breadth of his abilities. They wouldn't understand.

For he could fight like no mortal could.

In the madness of that slaughter, Azrael held nothing back; he employed all his martial skills. His strength. His speed and agility. And even a bit of the old magic.

He twisted and whirled.

He evaded.

In the chaos, he lost track of Lady Dahlia.

And of Pennebray.

All he saw were claws and fangs coming at him from all directions.

All he heard were grunts and cries, screams and maniacal laughter from all about. There could be no victory for Azrael in that place. The numbers against him were too great.

There was only death or escape.

It was not his nature to run. But even less so to die. There were too many infected. Far too many even for him to deal with.

And he was alone.

Every door, closed. Even the servant's entrance. Likely barred. No time to break through.

A window would serve.

4

THE DEAD FENS, THE KEEP

Year 1242, 4th Age
12th Year of King Tenzivel's Rule

Muscle, sweat, and Par Talbon's magic raised the portcullis but two feet more before it stuck again, the mechanism hopelessly jammed.

"That's it," said McDuff. "On your bellies and under. Quick!" he said as he glanced back whence the shamblers came. "They're on us! Get through, now!" he said as he shouldered past the others. He moved toward the shamblers, axe and shield in hand. He'd cover his comrades' backs.

Aradon and Malvegil both turned from the gate, prepared to stand and fight.

"Remember the hare," said Artol. "They'll pull us down. We've only a moment!" He grabbed Aradon by the arm and urged him toward the gate. As huge as Artol was, if Aradon didn't decide to move, he couldn't have moved him. Reluctantly, both lords scooted under the gate, Artol and Karktan following on their heels. A close fit it was, but the gate was just high enough for them to crawl under without fear of getting stuck.

A moment later, one shambler charged McDuff at a headlong sprint. Another veered toward Donnelin. The priest had no time to get under the gate, slowed as he was by injured ribs. Those two shamblers were far out in front, but their fellows followed in their wake, howling and croaking as they came.

McDuff sidestepped the creature; shield-bashed it as it went by. Its momentum diverted, but unbroken, it crashed head first into the portcullis at full speed. Bones broke with a sickening crunch. Its nose was staved in, though no blood from it flowed. It neither cried out nor showed any sign of pain.

McDuff spun toward it and slashed its throat with his axe before continuing his turn to meet the next attacker. That cut would have sapped the strength of any normal opponent and bled them out in seconds, but not the shambler. It ignored its wounds and started forward.

Just as the shambler poised to leap onto McDuff's back, Aradon's sword thrust skewered it through the back and held it fast. Karktan lunged forward, reached through the bars, stretched to his limit, and grabbed the shambler's hair. He pulled it back against the bars. His massive knife sawed three times back and forth across its neck before he severed its spine and the creature went limp.

The other shambler caught Donnelin in the midsection at a full run. It crushed the priest to the ground beside the entry and knocked the wind from him. The pain from his already damaged ribs was agony. His head spun. His vision dimmed. He was on the verge of blacking out. The creature's jaws snapped over and over: click, click, click. Its hands tore at Donnelin's cloak, lusting for his flesh, trying to bite his torso. So single-minded were its bites, it failed to go after his face and neck — exposed, easier prey, only inches farther away. Donnelin's arms jerked and spasmed, but he had no control of them, no strength at all; he couldn't even breathe.

In moments, the shambler shredded the priest's cloak and jerkin, but could do nothing against his chainmail shirt. Its jaws clamped on the mail with the force of a mad hound, but it received naught for its efforts but broken and splintered teeth. In the moments that took, Donnelin caught a breath; his strength began to return.

He grabbed the thing by the hair and forced back its head — calling on every ounce of strength he possessed. His other hand buried a dagger in its throat.

But it had no effect.

None at all.

The thing continued its flailing, its jaws snapping.

Donnelin yanked the dagger back, and then struck again. This time, he sent the blade up under the creature's jaw. The dagger sank deep.

And deeper still. Up into the thing's brain.

The shambler shuddered and twitched for several moments. With a moan, it expelled the last of its breath. Then it fell limp. Whatever infernal spark of life that possessed it, forever fled.

"Get inside," shouted McDuff to Donnelin as he stepped forward and met the charge of next wave of shamblers.

Not far away, Par Talbon held out his arm and pointed his right hand at an onrushing shambler. He mouthed secret words — war wizard words. Words known only to those few masters of the Tower of the Arcane's Pentarkian Order. Words that Par Talbon of Montrose knew all too well. Old friends of his were they; reliable, often visited, and always welcome.

Drawn from the ether by those words of power, a speck of blue light appeared in Talbon's palm. A tiny pulsating light, of no more consequence than that of a firefly. But it quickly grew.

In a moment, it expanded into a blue translucent sphere of half a foot in diameter. It held that size for but a second. Then it shot toward the shambler. Launched by Talbon's will, it buzzed and sparked as it flew. The magical sphere sped the ten feet to the shambler while coruscating streaks of white lightning erupted within its depths. It struck the shambler's head — and exploded — blowing it into a thousand bits that flew off in all directions. The shambler's body flopped to the ground. But the thing was not immediately done, not instantly dead. Its head gone, it thrashed violently about on the ground for some moments before finally it went still.

A second blue sphere of light appeared in Talbon's palm. It grew and shot from his hand just as the first, only quicker. It blasted into the chest of another shambler that charged McDuff. The eight inch diameter hole in its chest (all the way through and out its back), the edges of which were afire, didn't even slow it. It didn't even seem to notice the terrible wound.

McDuff's axe crashed into the side of its head and blasted it to pulp. It dropped, twitching.

More blue balls of energy sped from Talbon's hand in rapid succession, appearing and growing much quicker than the first. At first there were five of them. Then, a moment later came more. Ten, fifteen, twenty in total before Talbon reached the limit of his magics. Start to finish, the barrage took but a handful of heartbeats.

Each sphere unerringly struck a shambler in the head or chest. Each exploded and tore its victim to pieces. Those struck in the head dropped. Twitching or thrashing notwithstanding, they were out of the fight. Those struck in the chest were unfazed, no matter the size or severity of the wound — unless the blast severed their spines.

To the shamblers, spinal wounds were effectively fatal. They'd fall and shudder, their movements uncoordinated and erratic. Sometimes, they soon went still, apparently dead. Other times, they kept on shuddering and twitching until someone came along (however long that took), shattered their skulls, and crushed their brains.

"Get in here," yelled the others from behind the portcullis, for McDuff, Talbon, and Donnelin were still in harm's way. Despite Talbon's efforts

— a score or more shamblers down — on yet came more. Far more than they had thought.

Dozens more of the things loped toward the keep, only seconds behind the others. They picked up speed as they drew closer, transitioning into a headlong sprint while their croaking and gibbering grew louder and more frantic. The heaped and mangled bodies of their fellows failed to deter them.

Talbon backpedalled to the portcullis. Smoke rose from his hands. His arms shook. Blood dripped from his nose and ears. He set his back against the iron so that he could turn and retreat under the gate quickly as he prepared another spell.

"Get under," urged McDuff. "Both of you. I'll cover you."

"Get under," shouted the others.

Talbon saw that there were too many coming, and they were too close, moving too fast. They wouldn't all make it through in time. McDuff at least would be swarmed, maybe Donnelin too. The wizard raised his hands and touched his fingers together. "Duck," he shouted at McDuff just as a yellow wave of crackling energy erupted from his hands. The energy rapidly spread out in a line before him, humming and vibrating as it expanded. Like a low wall of pulsating, fiery energy it was. Then it launched forward.

It surged toward the shamblers and mowed them down like an enormous scythe through wheat, cutting them in two. It barreled through their ranks, row after row, slicing apart any and all it touched. A score or more shamblers went

32

down, never to rise again before the magic fizzled out and disappeared. He'd bought them a few seconds only, for more shamblers rushed toward them, only seconds behind the last.

Talbon staggered and dropped to his rump; his whole body shook as if in a seizure. His friends grabbed him and pulled him under the portcullis as acrid smoke rose from his hands. His fingers and hands trembled, fiery red at the palms, blackened at fingertips. His face was beet red and he grimaced in pain.

Donnelin pushed off the shambler that lay atop him. Somehow, the thing had life left in it. It held fast the priest's arm. Its fingers dug into his forearm and strained to pull it to its open mouth, jaws snapping: click, click, click.

Donnelin struggled to pull away. He beat the thing with kicks and punches to no avail. Every movement and breath agony due to his injuries.

McDuff slammed his boot into the shambler's head. That finally broke its grip on the priest.

Donnelin gasped for breath, unable to rise.

McDuff dragged him toward the portcullis. The shambler, still not done, crawled after them. "Get under," said McDuff to the priest.

"They're on you!" shouted Malvegil.

McDuff spun about, roaring; slashed with this axe; took the head from an unrushing ghoul. He swung again, a wide arc — sliced open the chests of two others; the force of the blows sent them reeling. He was out of time. Another mass of shamblers were but moments away, a dozen, maybe a score or more of them. They'd dive into him and swarm over him just as they'd done to the hare. No way to avoid that. They'd pull him down and that would be the end.

McDuff scooped up a fallen Lugron shield, turned toward the gate, and yelled "Make way." Holding the shield before him, he took three running steps and leaped forward. He landed belly down on the shield and slid straight under the portcullis, the ghouls not two steps behind him. Artol and Malvegil dodged out of the way and pulled Donnelin through just after McDuff slid by.

5

THE DEAD FENS, THE KEEP

Year 1242, 4th Age
12th Year of King Tenzivel's Rule

Two shamblers at the fore of the ghoulish pack dived onto Donnelin's legs, ripping and tearing, tooth and nail, frantic and frenzied to get to bare flesh. They came through with Donnelin, the ghouls did. Dragged along as the Lomerians pulled the priest under the gate. Donnelin flailed at them, foot and fist, desperately trying to knock the undead aside, but he failed to dislodge them, both his legs pinned good and proper.

The two shamblers went at Donnelin with filthy claws and gnashing teeth. They shredded his pants, but were thwarted by his long chainmail tunic.

Aradon crouched beside the priest, grabbed one shambler by the hair and, with his other hand, slammed a dagger into the base of its skull. The blade's tip erupted from the front of the thing's throat, but no blood followed it out. The shambler immediately went limp and lifeless.

Donnelin cursed the creatures back to Helheim, spouting phrases from some ancient ritual of exorcism that he only half remembered and had never performed.

The second shambler flailed maniacally, lost in a crazed frenzy, it scrambled up along the priest's torso, scouring his body for any unarmored spot in which to sink its teeth and claws. It roared a high-pitched howl as it drew near to Donnelin's face. The thing's putrid breath washed over the priest and nearly caused him to retch; bits of rotted flesh and foul spittle splattered across Donnelin's face.

His face twisted in fear and revulsion, Donnelin pressed his runic holy symbol against the creature's forehead. At the touch of that token, the creature's flesh sizzled and smoked as if touched by a hot iron. The shambler howled and jerked forward. It snapped its jaws: click, click — and then clamped down on both the holy symbol and Donnelin's hand. Its teeth, black and broken as they were, sunk deep. Deep into Donnelin's flesh. Its jaws like a vice.

Donnelin screamed.

He punched the thing with his right hand; its jaws locked on his left.

Blood spurted into the air.

Donnelin's blood.

Aradon pummeled the ghoul on the back of the head, once and then again; his fist struck with the force of a sledgehammer. Hard enough were those blows to dislodge the creature's teeth from Donnelin's hand, though the priest screamed at the impact, which tore ragged his flesh. Aradon grabbed the stunned shambler about the back of the neck, heaved it off the priest, and lifted it on-high with but one hand.

Eotrus thrust his sword through the undead thing's back. It flailed about, seemingly unharmed, and twisted its head around, trying to get at Aradon's hand.

To bite him too.

Its neck craned around farther than any man's neck should; far enough to chomp on Aradon's wrist.

But it never got the chance.

Artol's battle hammer slammed into the side of its head, blasting it to pulp. Aradon flicked what was left of the corpse off the end of his sword.

Just at that moment, the ghoul pack slammed into the portcullis at full speed. They crashed to a halt in a crunch of bones and maniacal howls. Even the stout steel of the gate strained and shuddered under that terrible onslaught.

But the gate held.

Thank the gods, it held.

The shamblers pressed against the bars in a mad frenzy; piled up so tightly against the gate (while more of their kind slammed into the rear of the pack) that those in front could not drop down to crawl under the bars, which still stood upraised two feet above the cobblestone pavement.

They stood there, those dead things did, roaring, croaking, and gibbering, arms desperately flailing between the bars, faces pressed up tightly against the iron, striving with all their might to push their way through, straining to get at the men beyond, their jaws snapping: click, click, click.

The undead covered every inch of the portcullis, blocking all view beyond. They climbed atop each other in their fervor to get at the Lomerians, with no regard for themselves or their fellows. They were out of their minds with madness: slavering, howling, spittle flying from their mouths. A surreal scene. Something from a hellish nightmare.

Above even the din of the dead, the Lomerians heard the frantic screams of several wounded Lugron who were strewn about the battlefield, out beyond the gate. The shamblers had fallen upon them, intent on devouring them. Despite all the wars they'd weathered, rarely had the Lomerians heard such screams — the agonized cries that men made while being eaten alive. A terrible thing to hear. Sounds to unsettle the soul and rattle the steeliest nerves. Sounds not soon forgotten. More stuff of nightmares.

The Lomerians, despite all their experience, froze for several moments, staring at their attackers, weapons in hand, braced and ready, expecting, fearing, dreading that the gate would topple.

That the shamblers would gain entry to the keep.

That they'd be overrun.

That they'd meet the same gruesome fate as the Lugron outside.

"Lower the gate!" roared Malvegil. "Ob, you bastard, bring down the gate!"

No sooner had he said that, when the chains that worked the portcullis rattled; the mechanism finally engaged. Ob had done it.

But the gate didn't head down.

It started to rise!

"No," shouted all the men.

"The other way," yelled Malvegil. "It's going up."

Six inches it rose, and kept rising. Soon the dead would pour through the portal, and charge them like mad things possessed.

"The gnome can't hear us," shouted Aradon over the din. He grabbed Karktan's arm. "Get to him. Lower the gate."

Karktan dashed off down the hall, splashing through the foul water as he went, shouting Ob's name.

Artol picked up a fallen spear and went at the shamblers that strained at the gates. He'd seen enough of them to know, blows to the head were all that worked. Anything else was useless. And even after headshots, sometimes, the dead kept coming. Relentless in their pursuit of flesh and blood.

Artol sent a powerful spear thrust through a shambler's forehead, deep into its brain. The thing dropped. Another thrust caught a shambler through the eye, and yet another thrust, impaled a third shambler through the mouth.

A moment later, Malvegil and McDuff were there, by Artol's side, stabbing and pounding more shamblers that pressed on the gates and those few that found purchase enough to crawl under.

The gate chains rattled and clanked. Another ghoul pulled itself under despite all the Lomerians' efforts to keep them out.

Aradon shouldered the shambler, knocking it back against the gate. In their frenzy, its own fellows held it fast for long enough for Aradon to bring his sword to bear in an overhand strike that sheared through the creature's skull.

Finally the gate moved down. Slowly. But down it moved. And when it sunk into the cobbles, and could move down no more, the Lomerians were safe at last from the dead.

For the moment.

No shamblers could get in; their way was blocked.

And the Lomerians could not get out.

6

THE HOLLOW

Year 801, 4th Age

Azrael ran toward one of the ballroom's big stained glass windows. He had no interest in jumping through it, but he had little choice. All other escape routes were cut off. Too far away were they. And too many of the things, the people he came to call, the "infected," barred his way.

The window was his last desperate chance for escape. They had him trapped good and proper, just as he feared when he arrived at Falstad Manor that night. He should not have let down his guard. A costly mistake.

He dodged past swiping, groping claws and gnashing teeth. He ignored the howls, the screams, the curses, and the blasphemies they threw at him.

Those black eyes they had. Inhuman it made them look. Like demons of legend. And so fast were they. So resilient. How had the serum done that to them?

And how had the contagion passed one to another? Thankfully, the infected had no skill at arms — common folk that they were, not that they needed much skill, not with those claws, those teeth, that preternatural strength. Terrible opponents were they. Fearsome. Bloodthirsty.

Wild to the point of madness and frenzy. And so many. Too many.

Hundreds.

He vaulted onto a table, claws swiping at him from all sides. He heard the cries of those few innocent folk still alive in the hall, still desperately fighting for their lives.

He turned from them. He abandoned them. He had to.

The great hero. The great Azrael the Wise. The last of the arkons of the lord. The Eternal.

He abandoned innocent folk to die horrific deaths. His neighbors. People he knew.

Even in that instant, that fleeting moment as he ran, fiends slavering around him, the guilt weighed on his heart and twisted his stomach to knots.

But he could not save them. Not even one of them.

All he could do was escape or die alongside them. Dying would serve no purpose. No good.

That he would not do.

And so he leaped for the window.

Crazy it was to try to jump through a window, head first, no less. Heroes always did that in stories, but in real life, it usually didn't work, and it always hurt. A lot.

As he launched himself forward with all the power his legs could muster, he didn't know what would happen. He half expected to bounce off the muntins, spindly as they were, and crash to the floor, the bloodthirsty horde all about him.

He closed his eyes, one arm outstretched holding his sword, the other protectively covered the top of his head.

Glass shattered and wood snapped. Glass raked his arms, his head, his clothing.

But he got through.

And fell into the night.

A cantrip he spoke — a single mystical word that slowed his fall. He rolled on impact with the ground, tumbling through some bushes, and avoided serious injury.

The battle had already spread to the streets. Azrael's guardsmen were there, fighting. Bloodied. Two men were down, infected atop them, straddling them. Biting. Tearing. And slurping at the blood that sprayed from their wounds. Like wild beasts they were.

The other guardsmen were hard pressed, but they didn't run, they didn't abandon their master, though Azrael would not have blamed them if they had, considering the things that came at them. Azrael felt pride at their loyalty and the good account they made of themselves in the fight, owing to their training, courage, and grit.

More than a few black masks followed Azrael out the window, howling and slavering like mad dogs as they went. In moments, Azrael and his men would be outnumbered several to one.

Azrael's sword took the head off one infected, a young man that he didn't recognize. Three of his guardsmen skewered another one.

There was no victory to be had. Not there. Not that night. Just as Azrael was hopelessly outnumbered and corned in the ballroom, soon he and his men would be entrapped on the grounds outside Falstad Manor. They had to flee.

Azrael called his squad together. They dashed down the walk, through the gates, and across the road into the shadows. Escaping into the night.

A few black masks stalked after them, though most stopped to feed on the fallen guardsmen. They covered them completely; swarmed over them like ants. A scene of horror.

7

THE DEAD FENS, INSIDE THE KEEP

Year 1242, 4th Age
12th Year of King Tenzivel's Rule

Ob and Karktan appeared as the men backed down the corridor, away from the portcullis and the howling mob of the dead that strained against it. The gnome was battered and out of breath. His clothes were soaked, his beard, dripping.

"You been swimming, Too Tall?" said McDuff.

"Odd," said Artol. "His annual bath is not due for a month."

"Mostly, I've been enjoying tea and crumpets with a bunch of stinking Lugron," said Ob as he displayed his bloody axe blade for the men to see. He looked past the others toward the gate, concern on his face. The moaning of the shamblers that massed there was loud and oppressive. "Lots of them left, I see."

"Is the portcullis mechanism secure?" shouted Aradon.

"It's held fast," said Ob. The gnome noticed that Donnelin was hurt and rushed to his friend's side.

"Artol, get Donnelin up," said Aradon. "We need to get farther away from this gate."

45

"You think they can get through it?" said Malvegil as he looked toward the gate. The shamblers were still pressed so tightly up against the bars, that had they been living men, the press of their fellows may well have killed them. Still they reached through the bars and flailed about, straining to reach the Lomerians in the corridor despite being hopelessly far away. Their jaws repeatedly snapped on naught but empty air before them; their clicking sounds nearly eclipsing their incessant howling and croaking. The mass of them still so thick that there was no view past them at all.

"I doubt it," said Aradon. "But I'm hoping that once we're out of sight, they'll move on. I don't want to fight our way through them to get out, especially not if we have to get out fast."

"Aye," said Malvegil. "I wouldn't want to be trapped between them and whatever else is behind this mess."

Aradon extracted a torch from a nearby wall sconce. "Take the torches," said Aradon. "They may be of use deeper inside. And with this corridor dark, maybe those things will disperse."

The men waded through the brown, putrid water, down the torchlit passageways that burrowed deeper into the keep and stank of death, decay, and worse. The torches revealed black mold that creeped up the walls and across the ceilings. Water dripped from everywhere. Stalactites of myriad sizes hung from the ceilings, formed from salts leached from the keep's stone over ages unknown. Paint flaked from the walls and flapped with the breeze of the Lomerians' passage.

The water-filled passages and the need for torches made it hard to move quietly through the place. The ripples in the water created by every step that they took made it impossible to move undetected.

Moaning and croaking sounds came and went, but the echoes in the place made it impossible to tell from which direction the sounds came. So they couldn't tell for certain whether what they heard was the shamblers outside, or others within.

Lugron corpses floated here and there; the walls and ceilings nearby splattered of blood, a red tinge to the water. "Gabe's been busy," said McDuff. The dwarf lifted his axe on-high and slammed it into the closest floater. "Best to be sure. Lugron are famous for playing possum."

"Some of them are my work," said Ob. "Mister Bigshot only took out the brash striplings what was eager for battle. Left the cagey veterans for me to deal with."

"I hope you left a few for us," said McDuff. "My axe is still thirsty."

"I've had my fill for today, thank you," said Artol.

"I haven't," said Malvegil. "I'll see every stinking Lugron in the place dead for what they did to Red Tybor and Master Gorlick. We never should have come into this bog with so few. I'm a damn fool to have gotten us into this."

"We need to keep alert, men," said Aradon. "We're still in the thick of it here, until I say that we're not, so we need to keep quiet — as quiet as we can."

When they rounded the corner at the end of the second passageway, they came upon a dead Lugron, his body draped over a short flight of steps that led up to an alcove that housed the lever and gears that worked the portcullis. Another Lugron lay freshly dead there. The alcove's window provided a clear view of the entryway and the shamblers that still crowded against the bars, thirty or forty strong.

"These two jumped me," said Ob, "but I gave them what for. Amateurs."

The alcove was the only dry spot they'd seen so far within the keep. They paused there to see to their wounds, which were mostly bruises, and minor lacerations.

The worst was Donnelin's hand and ribs. His hand was mangled and bleeding, but all the fingers were still there. Artol and Ob examined it.

"I can't believe Red Tybor is dead," whispered Ob as he pulled out his flask and Artol fished bandages from his pack. "And Gorlick too. Two of the best ever."

Ob poured a generous amount of the alcohol over Donnelin's wound and then Artol tightly wrapped it with the bandages. Donnelin weathered it all without a word. He just sat there, staring at his injury. Aradon and Malvegil looked on in silence. Talbon sat on the steps wringing his hands, his eyes glazed over. McDuff and Karktan kept watch.

"Red Tybor killed the Lugron leader," Ob told the men. "A big, one-eyed graybeard, quick as a gnome, and strong as an ox. But Tybor cut him down to size, right and proper. Then some backstabbing scum got him — a giant Lugron, big as I've ever seen. Hit the Pict from behind with a big hammer and—"

"Damn the Lugron, one and all," said Malvegil. "A scourge on all Midgaard, they are, and always have been. We need to wipe them out to the last, and be rid of them, once and for all."

"Did anyone see what happened to Master Gorlick?" said Artol.

"He came to a bad end," said Ob. "Not one he deserved."

"They took him," muttered Donnelin. "Not Gorlick anymore."

"What do you mean?" said Artol.

Donnelin only shook his head.

"He became one of them," said Malvegil, bitterness in his voice. "One of the shamblers. One of the dead. I saw it. I saw him turn; I fear I'll never forget it."

"I saw it too," said Donnelin. "He wasn't Gorlick anymore. A Lugron choked him out. He was dead. But then he opened his eyes and when he did, he was one of them. He bit the Lugron's neck. Tore out his throat like a crazed dog."

"It was his wound," said Aradon. "That bite on his arm that festered. It was killing him. If not for the Lugron, he'd have been dead before sundown anyways. And when he died in the battle, he came back. He came back as one of those things."

Artol stared down at Donnelin's bandaged hand.

"The dead coming back to life?" said Malvegil. "It's insane. Utterly insane."

"I'm a dead man," said Donnelin. He held up his arm, the bandage already growing red. "This bite will kill me, same as Gorlick."

"We don't know that for certain," said Malvegil.

"We know it sure enough," said Aradon. "If the wound festers, we'll know for certain."

"Donnelin would never betray us, my lord," said Artol. "He'd never attack us."

"I'd have said the same for Gorlick," said Malvegil. "But he went for Donnelin, fist and teeth, and would have killed him, if I hadn't been there to put him down."

"You killed Gorlick?" said McDuff bristling.

"He had to," said Ob. "And if he hadn't, I would have. Like the priest said, he wasn't Gorlick anymore. He was one of the dead."

"This is all crap," said McDuff. "You're all daft."

"Ob's right," said Donnelin. "Dear gods," he said shaking his head. "You should kill me now, before it's too late. One clean stroke to the head and then it'll be over. You'll do that for me won't you?" he said, looking to each man in turn. "I've looked after you men when you've been wounded – every one of you. I'd not let you suffer; not like this. Please. Do it. Do it quick."

"Dammit, we've no time for this," said McDuff. "Gabe is in here on his own and may need us. We've got to move."

"Do it," pleaded Donnelin. "I don't want to become one of those things."

"His arm," said Malvegil. "The bite is only on his hand. It hasn't begun to fester yet. If we cut it off, the sickness may not take."

"Maybe so," said Ob. "But a hard choice that is. We don't know that it will fester. We might take the arm for nothing. Might be best to take his chances."

"We know it will fester," said Aradon. "We know because of all of them outside. So many. Every crewman on those missing ships must have turned, and others too, to total so many of them. That means any bite, maybe even any scratch from those things means death. Otherwise, so many wouldn't have turned."

"Aye," said Ob. "Them words make sense to me." He turned his gaze to Donnelin.

"Better off one-armed than dead," said Donnelin after but a moment's thought. "Do it. Do it now."

The men looked to Aradon.

He nodded his agreement.

"I'll do it," said Ob. "The rest of you'd probably miss and take his foot instead." Ob pulled a flask from his pack. "Drink this, old friend. Every drop, quick as you can. Gnome whiskey that be. I don't part with it lightly."

Donnelin drank it down, coughing sporadically along the way.

"Where's your rum?" said Ob to McDuff.

McDuff pulled a silvered flask from his belt. "A few swallows of this on top of Ob's whiskey and you'll not be feeling nothing."

Donnelin gulped down half the flask. They waited a few minutes, the wailing of the shamblers at the gate oppressing them the entire time. Donnelin lay on his back, his arm hanging free over one of the steps.

"Hold him still," said Aradon.

Ob readied his axe.

Aradon put his hand on Ob's shoulder. "It's my place to do this thing." He took Ob's axe.

"My lord—" began Ob.

"No," said Aradon as he gestured for Ob to be quiet. "I will try to do this in one blow," said Aradon to Donnelin. Artol stood by with a torch to cauterize the wound.

"Odin, give me strength," said Donnelin. They put a piece of wood in the priest's mouth for him to bite down on.

One blow did it. It went through the priest's arm and smashed hard into the stone step, notching the axe and sending sparks flying. Aradon grabbed the torch from Artol and cauterized the wound. Then they wrapped it as best they could.

Through it all, Donnelin never passed out. The wood snapped in his mouth when Aradon put the flame to his stump, but the priest stayed with them. They replaced the wood, if only to keep Donnelin as quiet as possible. They gave him the rest of McDuff's flask. Then several long mouthfuls from a wineskin. After a few minutes the priest was composed enough that they could continue. Artol and Karktan stood on either side of him and carried him along.

8

THE HOLLOW

Year 801, 4th Age

"To the manor," shouted Azrael to his guardsmen as they regrouped outside Falstad Manor. He and the six that were left raced for home. As best as Azrael knew, no one else not infected made it out of Falstad Manor alive that night. All those that he left behind, died, save for some few that the creatures captured and infected with their contagion, turning those goodly folk into bloodthirsty killers like themselves. Into creatures of the night.

Azrael's group weaved a frantic path through darkened streets as the town alarm bells began to peal — first, the one at the Odinhome, and then that of the constabulary.

Three tolls of the bells meant fire — common enough, known to all. But that night, the bells tolled five times. Five tolls, repeated again and again, a brief respite between, meant that the town was under attack. Rare was it that such warning bells rang in The Hollow. Few in town were old enough to have heard the five bells afore. Fewer still were there when the sun rose the next morning.

How the alarms were raised so quickly, Azrael never knew. But one thing was certain. The alarms caused more harm than good. On hearing the bells, citizens poured from their homes to see what went on. Most did so unarmed, confused about the meaning of the five bells. Outside, in the dark, they were all too easy prey for the infected that swarmed into the streets that night from Falstad Manor to hunt. To kill. To feed. And to breed more of their unholy kind.

Halfway to Azrael's manor, which was called Virent Hall, all sign of pursuit fled. The infected that chased them, no doubt, stopped along the way to partake of easier meals. Azrael's group shouted to the folks that they passed to get inside. To arm themselves. To bolt their doors.

Some listened.

Many did not.

Azrael wanted to save them. To protect them.

All of them. And he would have, if it were within his power. But he knew he couldn't. He had to get home. Secure the place. Hunker down behind his defenses until he decided on the best course of action. He was not a man to take bold action without first thinking it through, without exploring all contingencies.

It was not long before the constabulary bells fell silent. The infected must have reached the station house. The lone marshal on duty overwhelmed. Like so many others that night, the poor soul would have had no idea what was going on. What those things were that were trying to kill him.

When Azrael arrived at the secluded lane where stood Virent Hall, he found it untouched and far removed from the night's events. In earshot of the town's alarm bells was it, but too far away to see what went on there.

Even as Azrael's group strode up the cobblestone walk to Virent Hall, the Odinhome's bells fell silent. Brother Jarkin would not have gone down without a fight — an old soldier of the Lomerian guard was he, retired to The Hollow some years back.

Refisal, Marple Butler, and Azrael's remaining guardsmen awaited them on the porch, weapons to hand, faces brightened at the sight of their master.

Azrael ushered them all inside and ordered the doors and windows closed, locked, and barricaded. No admittance to any; no door or ground floor window to be opened without his direct permission. No one dared defy his will on that. Not when he took the tone that he did. And not after the guardsmen told the others of the horrors that they'd witnessed in town.

With everything locked and barred, Azrael was confident that Virent Hall was secure, at least for that night. He had long ago hardened the place to resist unwelcome incursions, not that such things were known in The Hollow.

In fact, they were quite unknown.

But Azrael was a cautious man. A man that liked to be prepared for all possibilities.

The main door of Virent Hall was solid steel, overlaid with wood, expertly balanced to conceal its massive weight. Iron shutters covered every window, inside and outside, bolted and barred. The side and back doors were equally reinforced. The manor's outer walls, stout and solid stone, three feet thick up on the second floor, five feet thick at the first. There was no obvious weak point in Virent Hall's construction to exploit. It wasn't a fortress by any means, but it was as secure as a manor home could be.

Even so, Azrael wished that he had more men at his command. Many more. He wasn't yet certain of what was coming, or how this all would play out. But he knew at once that he couldn't put down this storm alone.

Azrael took to the second floor balcony, the one that overlooked the front of the house and had a goodly view of the lane. He'd watch from there. Refisal was at his side.

From its perch on high ground Virent Hall had an expansive view. Farm houses and manors were visible here and there, most closer to town, a few farther. They all seemed quiet. What Azrael could see of town was different.

Buildings were burning.

Not many. Just a few, here and there. No pattern to it.

Worse, he heard the screams.

A typical man's hearing would not have detected them at that distance, but Azrael heard them: the yells, the screams, and the pleadings of townsfolk.

He heard them dying.

He heard The Hollow dying.

Refisal heard some of it too. The infected were out there, hunting, killing, breaking into homes, attacking innocent folk on the streets. Killing on sight.

At first, Azrael expected refugees. He had men stationed at the front door, ready to open it on his command should any townsfolk come calling, seeking aid and shelter. Seeking sanctuary.

But no one came. He couldn't understand it at first. But then he realized, the townsfolk didn't see him as a protector. They didn't see Virent Hall as a place of refuge.

He was the town hermit.

The mad old alchemist, rarely seen and seldom spoken to.

Why would they go to him?

They'd seek out the constable and the town marshals, but they were already dead, the whole lot of them.

Azrael would have let the people in if they came. The townsfolk. He would have checked them, he and Refisal, as best they could, to route out any infected that sought to infiltrate, though, at the time, he knew not how he'd accomplish that. But he'd do his best. He'd save the people that he could. As many as he could. Even at the risk of letting infected into his home. He'd save what lives he could.

But no one came.

Not one.

Not to the mad old hermit's house.

"Part of me wants to storm out into the night, all geared and armored, magics readied," said Azrael to Refisal. "And hunt them down. All of them. Kill them all."

"But you won't," said Refisal. "Why?"

"How can I?" said Azrael. "Besides the fact that there are too many of them, I made them as they are. I am responsible for their condition. They're sick because of me. How can I kill them for it?"

"You've already killed more than a few of them tonight," said Refisal.

"Only in self defense," said Azrael. "They gave me no choice."

"You cannot let this slaughter continue," said Refisal. "Not if you have any power to stop it. But alas, I fear even you do not."

"I may find a way to reverse this," said Azrael. "A cure for it."

"That will take time," said Refisal.

"And it won't bring back those innocent folk that they kill in the meantime," said Azrael. "There's no good ending to this, as far as I can see."

"Lomion City will send troops when they hear what went on here tonight," said Refisal. "They will come in force, and put down the infected. It need not all fall on your shoulders, Master."

"Military help is much, much too far away," said Azrael. "And ill prepared I think to deal with the likes of these infected. By the time a large enough force arrives, the contagion will have spread far and wide. It may be unstoppable."

"The ridiculous irony of it all," said Azrael. "In my quest to atone for the last apocalypse, I may well have started another."

"Then what will you do?" said Refisal.

"I will hunt them," said Azrael. "Capture them wherever I can. Restrain them somehow. Kill them only when I must. Then I will find a cure for this new plague that I've unleashed. I'll not rest until I do."

"A risky plan, Master," said Refisal. "With the disease spreading as it does, who knows how many of them there may be by morning."

"It must be done," said Azrael. "We will begin in the morning. For now, I will get some sleep. You and the men must do the same, for I'll need all your help with this endeavor."

"I'll have the servants stand the watch in shifts throughout the night," said Refisal. "When morning comes, every fighting man at our disposal will be ready to move."

9

THE DEAD FENS,
INSIDE THE KEEP

Year 1242, 4th Age
12th Year of King Tenzivel's Rule

Sir Gabriel ventured deeper into the tower until he came upon another stone stair, this one far narrower and far taller than the last. It spiraled up and up. He knew he was close to his goal. The Master of the Fens was near.

Even there, Gabriel heard the roar of battle outside: the clash of iron and steel, the shouted orders, the yells, the screams, and the pitiful pleadings of wounded and dying men. Gabriel couldn't make out the words, dulled by distance and muffled by the stone, but he knew what the voices said.

It was always the same.

Baleful cries of mercy and help me joined with calls for water, and pleas for the healer or the holy man. Oftentimes, they spewed curses, for strong young men decried their fate. They refused to accept it. They thought themselves immortal and the shock of their wrongness spawned venom like little else. Some called on the gods — beseeching their aid, asking for some boon, or cursing them to Helheim for forsaking them. Some few lamented their misdeeds. And here and there, a man begged for death, the pain or disfigurement of their wounds too terrible to bear.

It was always the same.

Every time that Gabriel heard those things, he fought within himself. Allow himself to be moved by the cries, and be distracted by them, or ignore them, and lose another tiny piece of his humanity.

He wanted to ignore the cries, the weeping, the wailing. Such was a warrior's training. But he never could. Granted, he was hardened to them; more than most soldiers. But he never forgot that the wounded were men. It didn't matter on which side of what conflict they fought — they had families, friends, loved ones.

They had value.

They mattered.

Well, at least most of them mattered. Some men were evil to the core. Some men had it coming.

Not because they were on the other side of the conflict. Not because their culture was different, their religion different, their loyalties, different. Some men's hearts were stoney and black, icy and bleak as the northern sea. Lugron suffered from that condition more than did most men. But not all of them were of that sort, not nearly.

The thick stone of the keep's walls dulled their cries. Relegated them to naught but background noise, but couldn't completely keep them out.

In contrast, inside the tower, all was quiet. Not silent. Old buildings are never silent. But it was quiet. The loudest sound, the dripping of water from somewhere on high. The droplets fell in steady streaks down the center of the spiral stair and plopped when they merged with the pooled water below. With walls and floors but bare and naked stone, the echoes in the place were eerie, the shadows deep. Nothing to dull what sounds there were but layers of dust and grime.

Up and up the stair did Gabriel climb; an endless spiral; a long eerie trek in the dim light that trickled down through the skylight at the stairwell's apex. Slowly, cautiously, quietly did he ascend. The battle sounds from outside long now gone, though whether from distance or that the battle was over, Gabriel did not know.

At last, the steps ended at a modest landing that stood before a metal door — as rusted and scarred as the rest of the place, wall sconces lighting the last flight up. The door was old. Decrepit. A worthless hunk of weathered iron. But still, it appeared solid, and served its purpose, for it guarded something of great value to someone. Something valuable enough to set six Lugron warriors to defend it unto death, and lock and bar the door behind them.

Nowhere to retreat. Hold the door or die in the trying. Those were the only choices for those six men, save surrender. An odd position for Lugron — not known for their bravery or their devotion to duty. They were selfish things, concerned more for themselves and for the here and the now, than for their fellows or even their own long-term good — flaws that were the downfall of their olden race, more often than not. Yet, those six did not run. They did not flee or falter. Neither did they bargain or bribe. They stood their ground. They held their positions even as Gabriel walked up the steps toward them, his boots ominously echoing with each measured step that he took.

Three of the six guards were little more than boys. Frightened but fierce, with too little appreciation for their mortality. Two others were veterans, steely eyed and determined. The last Lugron — the one at the back, was the one in command. He studied Gabriel's every movement: hand, foot, and weapons. No common Lugron was he.

He was their champion.

A graybeard with silver eyes that reflected light like the moons. The best of them was he. A born killer. And he'd been about that business for a long time. By his look, he hailed from one of the old bloodlines. A scion of those Lugron born of the deep mountains — the ones far to the north, beyond the Kronar Range. His people had haunted those lands since the days of yore, back farther than any could remember.

Their mountains never knew summer. They lived their lives ever burdened with snow and ice, frost and cold. A place where even giants feared to tread. Those barren lands bred hard men. Cold men. Ruthless men.

Some called his people, the Vhen — a name that legend made monster. The tales of them bespoke of creatures with superhuman powers: profound strength, uncanny speed, great stamina, and insatiable appetites. It was said that they hungered for the flesh of men, far more than did their pedestrian brethren from farther south. That they longed for flesh, the Vhen did. Raw off

63

the bone, torn of their own teeth. The eating of flesh consumed their every thought and supplanted all other desires. It was an all-consuming obsession — to the point that it drove them to madness.

Like most legends, the tales were more exaggeration than truth, but some truth was there in the telling. For the Vhen were a breed to be feared.

But Gabriel knew that they were not monsters. They were but a tribe of men. Desperate men from a desperate land that did what they had to do to survive. But men, they were, make no mistake.

Gabriel had faced them afore. More than once. He knew from the first that the man who stood before him was one of them. He had the look: the grayish cast to his skin, the thinness of nose, the lean but muscled frame. The irony of the Vhen legends did not escape Gabriel, considering the nature of the creatures that even now haunted (and hungered) at the entranceway of the keep.

The Vhen champion was scarred of face and body — from sword, axe, and claw. He held the others with him, their feet rooted in place, awaiting his commands.

Their eyes met when Gabriel reached the landing below. The young ones wanted to charge down the steps, howling their battle cries. A word from the Vhen held them back. He wanted to talk.

"Stand down," said Gabriel, his voice firm, unyielding. "The battle is lost. The tower is taken. Stand down and you will yet live."

"So speaks one man against six," said the Vhen in a harsh accent different from most Lugron. "We guard here by oaths sworn and monies paid. Our word is our bond."

"No one else need die here today," said Gabriel.

"No one will," said the Vhen, "if but you and yours break off your attack and leave this place."

"For whom do you stand the guard?" said Gabriel.

"The warlock is what we call him," said the Vhen. "We know him by no other name."

"Be he a wizard in truth or only in name?" said Gabriel. "Be he a necromancer?"

"I know not," said the Vhen. "But a wizard he must be. Has powers and such. Great power in him I sense."

"What of the dead things that lately roam the Fens?" said Gabriel.

"The restless dead, we call them," said the Vhen. "Draugar is their name of old. The warlock's creations, they are, though control them, he cannot. They are why we're hold up in this pit."

"I would have words with your warlock," said Gabriel.

"He speaks with no one," said the Vhen. "And to see him, you must first pass us. And that you will not do," he said with a cough. "I grow weary of your language. Your Volsung words pain my tongue and sting my throat. They clog my gullet; I'm done with them, but this bit more I will say. We will not let you pass; no matter the cost. Go back now and live. Or climb closer and die."

65

10

THE HOLLOW, EBERT COOK'S HOUSE

Year 801, 4th Age

The hunters crept up to Ebert Cook's house, silent as ghosts, hoping to catch him unawares. Two burly men wearing ill-fitting armor, blacksmiths by trade, heaved the battering ram into the cook's door, Azrael and the other hunters arrayed behind them, poised on their toes, weapons in hand, bristling for battle. The doorframe burst and collapsed inward with a crash when the heavy iron slammed into it. Quick as could be, the blacksmiths dropped the ram, dodged to the side, and reached for wooden clubs.

Just as Azrael was about to charge toward the door opening, Ebert stormed out of it, blinking and disoriented, his gate, unsteady, as if just woken from a deep sleep. His skin was pale and grayish, his eyes black throughout; white fangs bared — the bottom ones, huge and curved like tusks. His shirt and breeches were mottled brown and red from blood and gore, and smeared of excrement; his hair, matted with it. He shook with rage, his eyes wild, eerie, alien; they darted from one man to the next, blinking rapidly as he tried to get his bearings. "The heck you want?" he spat as he flexed his fingers before him, a razor sharp claw at the end of each.

Azrael's men tossed their nets.

Two, three, four nets dropped over the cook's head, each one alone weighty and strong enough to entangle and bring down most men. Ebert's claws went to work, slashing this way and that, as he roared all the while. In but an instant he'd shredded the nets, his strength far beyond any normal man. A moment more and he tore one hunter's arm to the bone. Just as quickly, he pummeled another into unconsciousness with a backhand to the head.

Ebert's head snapped to the side when Azrael's club crashed into it. He didn't even stagger or grunt. He simply dropped to the ground as a felled tree. Blood spilled from his mouth and dribbled from an ear, one tusk twisted, chipped, and cracked from the club's impact. The hunters pounced on him, bludgeoning him over and again even as he thrashed about, half conscious, trying to defend himself. They pulled out ropes to tie him up, just as they had with the others; hog tied and blindfolded was his fate.

Azrael stepped past the scuffle into the darkened house, torch in hand, Refisal not far behind, though the gnome halted at the entry. Azrael's broad shoulders filled the whole of the doorway. He looked little like the hermitish alchemist that attended Pennebray's party but a few weeks before. Even then, he stood out, tall as he was, a head over most men, cheeks and chin chiseled from stone, piercing blue eyes of bottomless depth. A man of unassuming disposition, yet quite impossible to overlook or to forget.

Now he stood in armor of strange and curious make: emerald green it was, helm to boot; angular metal plates, polished to a sheen and form fitting, wicked spikes welded here and there about torso, limb, and helm. Of what metal it was forged, and by whose expert hand, the others had no idea, for in the battles they'd weathered since the outbreak of the bloodlust, as the contagion had come to be called, Azrael had been hit by blows powerful enough to crush a man or cut him in two, yet that armor rarely dented and never so much as scratched. All the while, it safeguarded Azrael from grievous wounds. Armor worthy of Heimdall (the grand smith of the gods) himself.

For all its strength, the armor was light and hardly encumbered the alchemist at all. He moved about as if born to it. That puzzled the hunters, for some few of them were his guardsmen, and had trained with him for countless hours at Virent Hall, his armor worn, always common plate and chain. Never before had the men laid eyes upon the green nor heard tell of it; from whence it sprang they had no clue. That ethereal armor called to mind the faerie stories and old legends that bespoke of giants and immortal warriors that strode across Midgaard amongst common men in antediluvian days — during the Age of Heroes.

Strange to say, but the armor made him seem more god than man. A silly notion for learned men. Yet when the hunters stood at Azrael's side, the armor upon him, his great green trident in hand, they were inspired to greatness, their fears washed away, their courage emboldened, a grandness to their purpose. They knew with certainty that they would not be defeated so long as Azrael stood with them.

The smell hit Azrael hard on the way into the cook's house. He knew what the torchlight would reveal, yet even that knowing didn't prepare him for what he saw. A sight to haunt the days and plague the nightmares of any sane man to the end of his days.

Azrael cringed. The hair rose on the back of his neck. Bile rose in his throat; he fought to keep it down.

Every surface of the home was splashed of dried blood and putrefying gore. Dismembered human body parts lay scattered about the floor and atop the kitchen table — the sorry remnants of Ebert's wife and his six children, infant to teen.

His own family!

Each one, butchered — mutilated without mercy or reason.

The work of a madman.

What evil could drive a man to such acts? What monstrous disease had Azrael birthed in that cursed serum? Of all the horrors Azrael had seen since the outbreak began, that house was the worst.

In Ebert's kitchen, atop the stove, a huge stew pot bubbled and steamed; the pungent odor of vegetables, herbs, and spices battled with the putrid smell of death. A heap of excrement two

69

feet tall sat in one corner of the room. Flies buzzed everywhere.

Azrael wanted no part of that slaughterhouse. Neither did the others. The hunters remained outside, one and all; more than one vomited from the stench that wafted out the cook's doorway. Even Refisal would not pass the entry, though he stood there stoically, almost comical looking with wooden club and overlarge armor, ready to aid his master if needed, his eyes focused on Azrael rather than the horrors about the room.

Azrael had to search the place, though he was loath to do it. He had to make certain that there were no other infected lurking within the house, and no innocent captives that yet needed freeing. It was his duty, or so he felt. So he did it. He moved tentatively about the place, trying not to make a sound and more importantly, not to slip, for the floor was slick with blood, entrails, and worse. He searched each room of the small place, opening every door, every cabinet, every hidey hole.

Then Azrael tentatively approached the stove. He went there last.

He didn't know why he had to look. Morbid curiosity perhaps. Whatever the reason, he had to look.

So he raised the lid and peered inside, and when he did, he gasped and reeled backward until his back slammed into the wall, his mouth open, shock and horror on his face.

The pot's lid dropped from his hand. It loudly clanged when it hit the floor. It spun and vibrated;

finally, after many moments, it went still and the place was quiet again.

What Azrael saw within that pot, no man ever knew. Not one of the hunters dared to ask. Not even Refisal.

"Burn it down," said Azrael, his voice strained, barely more than a whisper. "Burn this damned charnel house to the ground. Now."

11

THE DEAD FENS, INSIDE THE KEEP

Year 1242, 4th Age
12th Year of King Tenzivel's Rule

The parlay over, Gabriel readied both sword and shield. He climbed one step and then another.

The Vhen unleashed his men, the boys in the lead. They charged down the stair roaring curses. Though they were as swift as most men, to Gabriel, they moved as slowly as snails.

He thrust his sword into the abdomen of the first, bashed the second's head with his shield — the man tumbled down the stairs, dead before he crashed to a stop. The third's wild swing overbalanced him; Gabriel ducked, grabbed his ankle, and effortlessly heaved him over the rail, dropping him down the center of the stairwell.

The screaming didn't stop until he struck the bottom.

The veterans came next. Surprise on their faces; they didn't expect the youngsters to fall so fast. But it didn't deter them. They roared forward, fire in their eyes. They fought as a team: each swing, each thrust, timed together, simultaneously striking at different areas.

That caught Gabriel off guard. And they struck with skill, speed, and power. Few men could have withstood their assault, especially considering that they had the higher ground. Gabriel fought defensively, taking their measure, biding his time. Then a lightning slash of his sword tore open one Lugron's knee. The other, momentarily distracted, lost an arm to Gabriel's overhead chop. After that, the battle was over.

Only the killing remained.

They didn't give up, those two veterans. Fought until their last breaths, which came directly, their curses echoing off the walls. Gabriel finished such things quickly. He had no desire to make his opponents suffer, and he would give no wounded cur his back.

Through it all, the Vhen merely watched, taking Gabriel's measure. He stood his ground, waiting at his post atop the stair, spear in hand.

When he was finished with the others, Gabriel slowly ascended the steps, his sword and shield held close.

"You are the one called Gabriel?" said the Vhen in Lomerian.

Gabriel was surprised to be recognized. "I am."

The Vhen smiled. "I knew it had to be you. The speed, the skills. A legend you are. Hated. Feared. By my people, by the Lugron, and many others. More than a man they say you are. Part god they mark you in the tales."

Gabriel made no answer.

The Vhen shrugged. "True or not, a worthy opponent you be. The only worthy one that I have faced since coming south. I am Morgorlain, chieftain of the Stikdar Vhen, son of Gartak, slayer of Domis Darackti, and Lord of the Torg Peaks."

"Your name is legend too," said Gabriel, halting his movement up the stairs. "What does a Vhen war chief do with Lugron mercenaries?"

"My reasons are my own."

"Banished by your people, were you?"

Morgorlain's eyes narrowed.

Gabriel started back up the stairs.

"I've roasted men like you over winter's fire," said the Vhen. "Men the Lomerians named heroes. Men that thought themselves great. I've gnawed their bones and sucked out the marrow. Even now, their bleached skulls adorn my cave. The same fate for you, I promise," he said with an evil laugh. "A trophy, you will be. Just as the hundred like you that I've killed afore. Come now hero. Fall into my embrace."

Gabriel offered no barbs or taunts. He slowly advanced up the stairs. Never hesitated. Never showed any doubt or fear. That was his reply.

Morgorlain's thrust was faster than fast and packed with frightening power. Aimed for the narrow gap between Gabriel's shield and his sword, it bounced off the shield's edge and thudded against Gabriel's breastplate.

Both men were taken aback

The Vhen, that Gabriel deflected much of the blow, and that his armor held back the rest. Gabriel, that so swift was the thrust that he failed to catch it clean on his shield.

Then came the exchange.

Morgorlain's lightning spear thrusts struck high, then low, then at Gabriel's midsection.

Clang, clang, clang went the sound as Gabriel's shield blocked them all.

Again came the spear thrusts. Faster now. At this angle and that.

Very high.

Very low.

In a sweeping arc.

From every direction at once.

Over and over and over, the clanging like a metal drum played to a fast tune.

Clang. Clang. Clang.

Gabriel's sword and shield formed an impenetrable wall.

Gabriel bided his time, defensive movements only: parries and blocks. He made no attack.

Not a single blow.

The Vhen showed no sign of tiring, his endurance as severe as the long winters of his home.

And then at last, Gabriel's sword bit back.

It sheared the Vhen's spear in two.

Then Gabriel advanced, sword dancing.

Morgorlain dodged, spun, and cheated death, skirting Gabriel's deadly strikes. A long sword appeared in one of the Vhen's hands, a brutish dagger in the other.

Steel met steel.

Sparks flew and steel screamed. The weapons, too fast for any normal man to follow. Each man struck ten blows in half as many seconds.

Then it was over.

The Vhen slid down on his rump. Blood pumped from the deep slash in his neck. He put his hand to his throat, but he could not stem the tide. He tried to speak, but blood clogged his mouth. His cold eyes locked on Gabriel's and never blinked. The Vhen raised his hand in salute, a gesture of respect.

Gabriel nodded, but held his ground until no more blood spewed from the Vhen's wound, careful all the while that no other Lugron crept toward him in the darkness.

Then he waited some moments more.

Finally, Gabriel swung his sword and the Vhen's head parted from his neck. He gripped Morgorlain's ankle, pulled, and slid the body out of the way, down the steps, the treads slick with blood.

The iron door now Gabriel's next obstacle.

And then he heard them coming.

Booted feet sloshing through the water in the corridor below.

Many men.

There was no time to get through the barred door, if even he could get through it at all. Now it was Gabriel's back that was against the door. Nowhere to retreat.

Figures stealthily moved up the stair. So quiet were they, an ordinary man may not have even heard them. Gabriel estimated as many as ten. He'd be hard pressed to deal with that many if they were even half as skilled as the Vhen chieftain.

Gabriel took a deep breath and braced himself, thankful for holding the high ground this time. They rounded the stair's bend, the light of a fallen torch upon them.

12

THE DEAD FENS, INSIDE THE KEEP

Year 1242, 4th Age
12th Year of King Tenzivel's Rule

Finding a stair leading up, Ob and his group proceeded with caution but met no resistance. They peeked through a second floor doorway accessible directly from the stair. Within, a large storage room, devoid of life and Lugron, but filled with crates and boxes of all sizes. Ob scouted it while the others waited on the stair.

"Water, wine, foodstuffs, textiles, and whatnot," said Ob as he scurried back, stuffing a small wineskin into his pack. "All new, fresh, and Lomerian."

"The cargoes of the missing ships," said Malvegil.

"Stinking Lugron are behind it all," said Ob.

The stair ended one more flight up. The door at the top stood ajar; broken in, the frame shattered. Ob swung it open.

Within, a large room filled with rows of soiled cots, bunk beds, and moth-eaten blankets. It stank of sweat and worse. Six Lugron corpses lay strewn about the floor, fresh blood pooling about them. Four were near the entry, two others on the far side by an exit.

"Gabe's work," said Ob.

"Then where is he?" said Malvegil. "That door can't lead to much more than a closet."

But it did. It led down a dark corridor, up and down several flights of stairs that wound wildly about.

"A madman built this place," said Ob. "The layout makes no sense."

The corridors they passed through were dark and silent, damp and moldy. The stale air was oppressive; the men coughed and sneezed despite their need for silence; their eyes and noses, itchy and running. Only Ob and McDuff were unaffected; their people long accustomed to the heavy, damp air of caverns deep and dark. So those two took the point.

Doorways lined the corridors at uneven intervals; some with doors bolted or locked, others ajar, but most with no doors at all. The doorways stood as black chasms in which anything might lurk.

"Bust them in?" said Ob to Aradon.

"No," said Aradon. "It will take too long to get through all these. We find Gabe first and double back to these doors if there's a need. Peek in each door that's open, but waste no time about it, and don't enter."

Malvegil didn't look happy at these pronouncements but held his tongue.

They moved on. Ob and McDuff held torches and paused at each doorway, but they saw little, most of the rooms extending beyond the limits of their light. Everywhere they looked was long deserted.

"This place be a deathtrap," said Malvegil. "They could come at us at any time, from any of these rooms. We could have left a hundred behind us already. We may have entrapped ourselves."

"We may have," said Aradon. "But we've little choice in this, unless we leave Gabe to his own fate, which I will not do."

"He chose to go off on his own," said Malvegil. "That was reckless."

"Gabriel is his own man, as I said afore," said Aradon. "But I won't abandon him."

"You risk us all," said Malvegil.

"As I would for you," said Aradon. "And you for me."

"Aye," said Malvegil nodding. "That I would. But still, I don't have to like it."

After a time, they heard fighting in the distance. It seemed to come from ahead of them, but was muffled by the keep's twists and turns. They picked up their pace and soon came upon another stair, this one, a tight spiral leading up, reaching high. A dead Lugron lay mangled at the base, freshly fallen from on-high. Torchlight glowed from near the stairwell's top.

"I guess we're still headed the right way," whispered Malvegil as he studied the corpse. "Your boy is being quite productive."

Halfway to the top, the stair was slick with blood. Lugron corpses lay dead here and there. A lone figure stood in the shadows at the stair's apex.

13

THE DEAD FENS, INSIDE THE KEEP

Year 1242, 4th Age
12th Year of King Tenzivel's Rule

"**G**abe," hissed Ob as he bounded up the stairs, a smile on his face. He slowed as he neared the tall knight that stood at the top of the stair, to make certain that Gabriel knew it was him before he ventured within weapon range. Gabe looked little the worse for wear.

Gabriel smiled; his eyes flicked across the group as they came up the stairs behind Ob.

"Red Tybor?" said Gabriel. "And Gorlick?"

Ob turned away, not wanting to say the words.

"Dead," said McDuff.

"Drinking with Odin, even now, the both of them," said Aradon.

"Warriors' deaths they had, long to be remembered," said Malvegil.

Gabriel's eyes narrowed. The men all looked battered, especially Brother Donnelin. Gabriel's eyes lingered on the priest's stump. "A hard day," he said, "and not yet done."

"You've been busy," said Aradon gesturing toward the Lugron corpses.

"I lost count at twenty," said Gabriel. "They fought to the last to keep me from whatever lies behind that door. A Vhen was amongst them," he said pointing to the Lugron's corpse.

"A Vhen!" said Artol. He spat on the Lugron's body. Several of the others did the same.

Malvegil studied the fallen Vhen warchief, never having seen one of his kind before.

"Hopefully, that was the only one," said Aradon. "If the Vhen venture south in force, there will be hell to pay. We'll have another war on our hands."

"A rogue or outcast I think he was," said Gabriel, "though he would not admit it."

"Do you hear that?" asked Ob, his big gnomish ears twitching up and down as they were often wont to do.

"Yes," said Gabriel.

"Hear what?" asked Malvegil.

"Shamblers behind the door," said Ob. "Moaning and croaking the way they do. Not so loud as them outside. Maybe because they can't see us. But it's them. And there's more than a few of them, methinks."

"We're getting that door open one way or another," said Gabriel. "Whatever we find, whatever horrors we see when the door opens, we plow forward. We bring them down. I will see this done and over. These abominations must be put down, and their master with them."

"It's barred from within," said Gabriel to Ob as the gnome approached and examined the door.

"Magic Boy," said Ob to Talbon. "You got any mumbo jumbo what can pass us through this door?"

"I'm a sorcerer, not a burglar," said Talbon, his voice weak. His face was still unnaturally pale, his body jittery. He looked as if he were about to puke. "Maybe I can blast us through, but only if there's no other way."

"Why not just blast away?" said Malvegil waving him toward the door. "Knock it down, if you can."

Talbon shook his head, his eyes downcast. "I'm spent," he said. "If I pull any more from the weave today, you'll be carrying me too, if I'm lucky — if not, I'll be dead. Find another way through."

Malvegil looked shocked by the wizard's answer. That shock quickly turned to anger. "Find another way through, you say to the Lord of the Malvegils?"

"He'd blast it down if he could," said Aradon before Malvegil could speak further. "And he will, if all else fails."

"Aye, my lord," said Talbon.

Malvegil shook his head and looked at Aradon, disbelief on his face. Malvegil men did their duty and knew who was the boss. Aradon's men seemed to think themselves their lord's equal.

"McDuff," said Ob. "The duty falls to you, Red Beard. I've ten stinking silver stars that says you can't get through this door in as many minutes."

"I'll match that," said Malvegil. "And double it, if you get through within five."

"Done, and done," said McDuff with a smile.

"In the meanwhile," said Ob, "perhaps Mr. Wizard Boy should lie down and take a bit of a nap; rest his weary bones and restore his delicate constitution. Someone find him a fluffy pillow and a nice warm blanket. Maybe some slippers and warm milk too." Then Ob stepped up to the wizard, and lowered his voice so that only Talbon could hear. "Ask nicely, and maybe Lord Malvegil the Great will take off your shoes and rub your feet for you."

Talbon rolled his eyes and shook his head. He sat on one of the steps and leaned back against the wall. He looked as if he'd pass out at any moment. That, or else puke.

As McDuff studied the door from a few steps back, Ob put his ear to it. "They're not right up against the door," he said. "All the sounds are from well back."

"Getting through won't be quiet," said McDuff.

"Do what you must," said Malvegil. "Just get us through."

Ob pounded on the door and slowly ran his hand across its frame. "An inch thick. Solid iron. Stout frame, also iron." Ob shook his head and moved aside. "Good luck, Ginger Boy. You'll not get through that so easy."

"No room for a ram," said Malvegil. "Not that we have one."

"Not enough men anyways," said Ob. "If we get through it, it'll be by brains not brawn — unless them buggers inside decide to open up on their own."

McDuff stepped up to the door, his massive long-hafted axe in hand. He pushed against the door, and rapped on it all about its edges. He even had Karktan get down on hands and knees so that he could stand on his back and reach the very top of the door and its frame.

"We don't have time for you to court the darned thing," said Ob to McDuff. "Get to picking or whatever you're about."

"There's no lock on this side, so nothing to pick," said McDuff. He turned back to the others and smiled. "But that won't be stopping me, laddies." Still atop Karktan's back, he turned his axe backwards and rammed it haft first as hard as he could into the top corner of the door, opposite side from the handle.

Nothing.

Karktan groaned and nearly tumbled over. "You're breaking my back," he said.

"Stop your complaining, whelp," said the dwarf. Malvegil and Artol stepped up and steadied the two. Two more times did McDuff ram the axe handle to the same spot before the men heard the snap of metal.

"Hmm. Who'd have thought?" muttered Ob. "Broke the hinge. Snapped it clean, sounds like. Nicely done."

Four more blows and the lower hinge snapped as well. The door still held fast.

"They've set a bar across it," said McDuff. "Something stout, maybe wood, maybe iron. No matter."

"Why not?" said Malvegil.

"Because they had to anchor the supports for that crossbar into the stone wall on either side. I bet they didn't know how to do that, least not the right way. With the hinges busted, hit it hard enough and them bolts will pop."

"So we do need a ram," said Malvegil.

"I didn't see anything in this whole place that we could use," said Aradon.

McDuff chuckled. "I'm the ram. Everybody, clear out of my way."

With a running start and a dwarven roar, McDuff crashed shoulder first into the middle of the door. With a thunderous snap the door fell inward, McDuff atop it. Gabriel and Ob were through the doorway in an instant, weapons at the ready.

THE DEAD FENS, INSIDE THE KEEP

Year 1242, 4th Age
12th Year of King Tenzivel's Rule

As the iron door thundered down under McDuff's assault, a piteous cacophony of croaking and gibbering assailed the men's ears, and an overwhelming noxious charnel house fume flooded their noses. Here were horrors the like of which they had not experienced before, not even in their most fevered nightmares.

The room, part laboratory and part torture chamber, was in truth a vast chamber of horrors. A charnel house of blood and bones, death and undeath.

Shamblers, in various states of decay and dismemberment writhed on rows of bloodstained tables and benches toward each side of the room, held down by thick iron chains securely fastened with heavy bolts. More of their kind hung chained to the walls or dangled from the high ceiling, straining against their bonds, froth dripping from their mouths. Buckets of congealed blood stood beside the tables; heaps of putrescent gore collected about the floor.

As the Lomerians entered, the shamblers' eyes turned toward them. They stared at them.

They wailed and gibbered and moaned. They struggled and strained, trying to move toward them, slavering, drooling, their jaws snapping: click, click, click. But the Lomerians were safe for the moment, for every shambler that displayed any sign of life or locomotion was restrained, unable to move toward them and attack. So long as the men stayed beyond arm's reach, they could move reasonably safely about the room.

Bloody boot prints criss-crossed the stone floor. Large boots were they, but whether of Lugron (known for their large feet) or some other folk, was impossible to tell.

In one corner of the room sat a pile of innumerable dismembered arms and legs. In another, a heap of rotting corpses piled six feet high.

The room's center was congested with tables stacked with glass jars and vessels brimming and bubbling with strange fluids. Glass tubes and bamboo shafts connected many of the strange vessels together. Some sat on small platforms above burning candles, and bubbled and smoked. Surgical instruments of curious design laid about: knives, scalpels, clamps, and saws.

Ob helped McDuff to his feet, and the three warriors stood in horror just within the doorway.

"What madness is this?" said Ob. "Why torture the dead? To what end."

"They're experimenting on them," said Malvegil as he stepped inside behind the others.

"So it seems," said Gabriel as he scanned the room.

"To find out how best to kill them, you think?" said Ob.

"Or to create them," said Malvegil. "Or perhaps to cure them."

Gabriel started at this and turned toward Malvegil, a strange look on his face. "To cure them," he muttered.

"They're diseased aren't they?" said Malvegil. "At least before they died, they were. Like Gorlick; his infection. Perhaps some madman is trying to cure them."

"A madman all right," said McDuff. "No battlefield was ever so bloody. We'll find no one alive here, methinks."

"We must put an end to this place, and its master," said Gabriel, his voice cold and resolute. "Spread out, two to each side, and stay clear of the shamblers. Don't let them touch you or get their blood on you."

"There's blood everywhere," said Ob.

"Well don't touch it," said Gabriel.

They proceeded through the chamber, passing row upon row of the writing dead and table after table of vials and tubes and strange experiments, their nature unknown.

Par Talbon paused before the experiments, studying them.

"What make you of it?" said Aradon.

"This is beyond me," said Talbon. "Beyond anything I've seen. Even the instruments — their style and make and materials. What craft forged them, I cannot guess."

Talbon discretely snatched up various small vials and containers that had secure lids, and stowed them in his pouch. McDuff liberated several curious instruments and tools and dropped them in pocket and bag.

Gabriel reached the rear of the chamber, and having found no enemies (at least none that could reach them), he turned back toward the others. He noted McDuff's rummaging. "Touch nothing," he said. "Take nothing, on your peril."

McDuff dropped the strange metallic tool he'd just picked up, and stepped away from the table, though he did not empty his pockets. Talbon, already finished with his scavenging, also kept secret what he had found.

At the rear of the laboratory was an anteroom with a narrow stone stair that led up to yet another level. The floor at the base of that stair was damp. Several buckets lay in the corner. Some empty, some filled with water.

"They wash off their boots before going upstairs," said Ob. "How quaint."

"Can't be tracking blood everywhere, you know," said McDuff. "Even madmen have their standards."

True enough, there was no blood trail leading up the stair.

Gabriel pushed past McDuff to stand at the van. "Stay behind me," he said.

"What about these shamblers?" said Artol. "Shouldn't we kill them?"

"When we're done with the master of this place," said Gabriel, "we'll come back and finish them. For now, leave them be."

They proceeded slowly and carefully up the spiral stair, the skirling sounds eventually dampening out behind them. The stair wound up and up, fifty feet or more, dark and dizzying. At the top, an iron guardrail and gate closed off the end of the upper chamber from the stairwell. Gabriel climbed just high enough to peek over the edge of the stair wall.

The stairwell opened into a great hall, vast and foreboding. Here, sigils of the master of the place were plain to see — emblazoned on column, shield, and banner.

Unmistakable in their origin were those sigils. Yet Gabriel disbelieved. He paused, fingering his ankh, and studied those marks — every line, every detail. He needed to be wrong. He needed that sigil to be someone else's.

But he wasn't wrong. It was the sigil of Azrael the Wise, once an arkon of Azathoth in the days of yore.

How that could be, Gabriel didn't know. He cleared the thoughts from his head, lest they hinder him with what was to come.

15

THE HOLLOW, VIRENT HALL

Year 801, 4th Age

A construction site, a dungeon, an asylum, a mad house. To Azrael's horror, his manor had become all of those over the past weeks.

Before the bloodlust spread, the grand old house had long been his sanctuary. A quiet place of reflection and research, far removed from the cares of the outside world. He'd pass his days in seclusion, in laboratory and library, experiments smoking and bubbling, books piled high, no one to bother him, save Refisal. Only his duty to keep sharp his martial skills tore him away from his research for an hour or two, here and there, during each day.

The peace he'd found at Virent Hall, such as it was, was over. The place would never be the same. Now it was his own little slice of Helheim.

Even in normal times, he hated construction in his home. He could tolerate the noise, but he couldn't abide the dust soiling his things or the general disruption to his routine. All renovations were done while he was away; everything tidied up and in good order before his return. It took a bit of time for him to get things back in their proper places, where they were meant to be, but it was worth the trouble to keep his home in good order and pristine condition.

What went on in the basement was altogether different.

He'd had the blacksmiths, the mason, and their helpers working day and night for a ten-day, partitioning off the manor's basement and constructing cells.

Ten by ten foot cells.

Iron bars, braced and reinforced, sunk deep into stout mortar, the basement walls of solid stone, several feet thick.

His own dungeon, like the mad lords of song and story.

Despite the workmen's efforts, they couldn't build the cells fast enough, for the hunters brought in more infected folk every day. Captured, one and all, at great risk, and cost to life and limb.

In the days that followed the massacre at Falstad Manor, Azrael gathered many men to his side to stand against the infected and halt further spread of the bloodlust. He called the group, the hunters, for that was their function.

The hunters stalked the infected wherever they hid. They routed them out and captured every one they could. They killed all those that they couldn't capture. Azrael's own guardsmen joined him, of course, as did a squad of passing mercenaries under the command of the famed sword master, Jaros Tull. But the bulk of the hunters were local townsfolk: shopkeepers, farmers, tradesmen. Most with little or no skill or experience at arms. But they fought with purpose. To save their loved ones that had fallen victim to the disease.

Or else to avenge them.

One hunter had two brothers in those cells. Another's father was there. Another, his two grown children. Two others, their wives. They hoped that the great alchemist would discover a cure and restore their loved ones to health — to the people that they once were. They put all their faith in him.

Azrael made the hunters no grand promises, but he vowed to do all in his power to cure the afflicted. So they stood by him, the hunters did, and one by one, they died for it, for the infected were terrible foes: stronger, faster, and far more resilient than normal folk.

Where once there approached one hundred, only twenty hunters remained.

Azrael's basement, once wide and open, was now bisected by a corridor, cells to either side. Ten were occupied. Most by two of the infected. Some by three or four. Most of them had their hands chained behind their backs, the chains attached to thick iron rungs bolted to the stone walls. Others were hog tied and lay upon the floor helpless. Some few roamed their cells freely, having slipped their bonds — they were the most dangerous.

"I can't do it," said the sell-sword, his face haggard and drawn as he stood before the door that led to the basement. "Not another night down there. Not for all the silver in Shandelon."

"They're locked in solid," said Marple Butler. "They can't get out. There's nothing to fear, lad."

"I'm not afraid of anything," said the sell-sword. "I'll face any man in battle. I've faced those things in battle, right beside the wizard, almost since the beginning. And I will again. But the things they say," he said, his voice crackling. "The howling. The taunts. The threats. It's like they're in my head. Like they know my thoughts. They say just the right things to anger me, to unnerve me, to drive me mad."

"Did you use the wax to stuff up your ears?" said Marple.

"It doesn't work," said the sell-sword. "I can still hear them. It's like their voices are inside my head. Every time I'm down there, it gets worse. Like they're getting stronger. Smarter. Better at it. Or else, I'm getting weaker. I can't take it. Hours of listening to shouted blasphemies—".

"The whispers are the worst," said Azrael. "They kept it up for hours the other night. Spouting blasphemies. Cursing the gods. And promising every pleasure imaginable in return for their freedom."

"A difficult thing for any man to bear," said Azrael. "Perhaps you've borne enough, for a while at least. I will stand the guard in your place, tonight. You go get some rest."

The sell-sword nodded, thanked Azrael, and quickly took his leave.

"Master, you cannot remain down there night after night," said Refisal. "Too much of it will drive you mad. Let the other men take shifts. The burden cannot all be on you."

"Too late, I fear," said Azrael. "Madness has long nibbled at my toes. Now it has devoured me whole."

"Do not say that," said Refisal. "Rest. Sleep. That's all you need. That and some good food and you'll soon be yourself again."

"I don't even know who I am anymore," said Azrael.

"Let me stand the watch this night," said Refisal. "Go get what rest you can."

"No, my friend," said Azrael. "This burden falls to me."

16

THE DEAD FENS, INSIDE THE KEEP

Year 1242, 4th Age
12th Year of King Tenzivel's Rule

Gabriel slowly opened the iron gate at the top of the stair, careful to make no sound. He entered a dilapidated hall, large and high ceilinged — vaulted at its center, the others just behind him.

That hall had been richly furnished once, but its couches, chairs, and carpets were tattered and frayed, stained, torn, and decayed. Garbage lay strewn about the stone floor — papers, tools, broken glass, bits of rotted food. Cobwebs enshrouded the rafters and every corner and crevice, the whole place chill, damp, and close.

Tall windows encircled the chamber; cracks in the foggy glass offered a constant draft, however slight; the outside air, welcome, foul and chill as it was. The diffuse light that streamed into the place was unable to dispel the hall's pervasive gloom or lessen its shadows.

On one side, beyond the windows, was a wide terraced roof of stone that capped the broader tower below. Barren was that terrace, save for a lonely, weathered chair of wood that faced the west.

At the far end of the hall lurked an empty throne of cold gray granite. Monumental in size was that perch, adorned in geometric runes, its sides carved to spikes, once polished, though now dull and grimy; its back reached for the ceiling, runes aplenty.

On either side of the throne stood a stoic metal sentinel — a symbolic honor guard, ever-present beside their master when he held court. Each statue was forged in the shape of a tall, square-jawed and muscled soldier clad in exotic plate armor of emerald hue, their silver skin, once polished to a mirrored shine, now dulled of age and grime. In bygone days, those statues were masterpieces of metalcraft, but now they stood long neglected; corrosion slowly devouring them.

The hall stood empty of life, or so it seemed. Where lurked the warlock of which the Vhen spoke? Where lurked Azrael the Wise or his impostor?

In hiding? Waiting in ambush? Indisposed? Dead? Or a fiction from the start?

Gabriel knew not, but he saw at once that the hall was large, cluttered, and dark cornered — an easy place to hide any number of men, so he proceeded slowly, cautiously — wary of ambush and booby trap.

He had not gone but a few steps from the stair when a claxon sounded, long and deep. Gabriel froze, then crouched and looked about, but nothing stirred within the room. A moment after the horn fell silent, a strange, deep voice that came from everywhere and nowhere spoke but a single word. "Ten," it said.

Gabriel looked around, trying to locate the speaker, the others did the same, but there was no one. Nothing.

"Nine," said the disembodied voice after but a brief pause. Only then did Gabriel realize that the voice spoke in the old tongue — the common language of days long past, back unto the time of Azathoth. Long dead and forgotten was that language. Few alive could translate it in written form, fewer still by ear.

"What's it saying?" said Ob.

"A countdown," said Gabriel. "Get back down the stair. Go down to the next landing."

"Eight," said the voice as Gabriel searched about the hall's entry for any lever to pull, switch to flip, or secret panel to open.

"Why?" said Aradon.

"Because if I don't figure out how to shut it off, something—

"Seven."

"Bad will happen."

"Six."

Reluctantly, the men complied, though Ob hovered near the very top of the stairs, not wanting to miss a thing.

Gabriel was at a loss. There was no lever or switch to be found, unless skillfully concealed. He knew not what might happen when the speaker completed his countdown, but suspected it was nothing good. If not a lever, a password perhaps?

"Five," said the voice.

"Stop," said Gabriel in the old tongue. "Halt."

"Four."

"Azathoth; Azrael," he guessed.

"Three."

"Enter; friend; arkon."

"Two."

"Let me pass."

"One."

"Shit."

Gabriel backed toward the stair. For a few moments nothing happened. Silence ruled the hall. Suddenly, a metallic clanking and clattering sound rushed toward him from above and just behind, even as the floor vibrated below him. No time to look up, the metallic roaring growing in his ears, he dived forward and rolled, head over heels, just as iron gates slammed down behind him with a skirling crashing and banging of metal.

Dust filled the air, obscuring his vision, though he saw that the bars extended around the entirety of the stair opening, outbound of the guardrail, precluding his escape from the hall, and cutting him off from the others. The bars fell from on-high, the trap doors of their origin concealed behind ceiling soffits. Had his reactions been but an instant slower, Gabriel would have been skewered by the spiked metal posts as they crashed to the floor.

The iron of those bars was two inches around, solid and strong, forged in flame in times long past. Not more than eight inches stood open between them. Too close to squeeze through; too thick to hope to bend.

A skirling noise of metal grinding against metal erupted from far across the hall — from nearby the throne. At the first sound of it, Gabriel feared he knew its source, but hoped that he was wrong. He spun toward it.

The two metal statues beside the granite throne were no longer still as stone. No mere decorations were they. They were moving as if alive. And they looked in his direction.

"Oh, shit," said Gabriel as he unconsciously backed up against the bars.

Ob peeked up and over the stair's edge, coughing, cursing, and covered in dust and bits of stone.

Gabriel turned his head toward the gnome. The great knight's eyes were wide. Was it surprise? Alarm? Or was it fear? Ob knew well that Gabriel feared nothing, so it couldn't be that. "Get these bars up and quick," said Gabriel.

The gnome looked past him, deeper into the hall. He saw them. The statues. Moving.

"Oh, shit."

17

THE HOLLOW, VIRENT HALL

Year 801, 4th Age

Azrael sat the stool in the middle of the dungeon's corridor, between the new cells under construction and those already occupied.

He hated the dungeon.

Every time he entered the place he wanted to puke. The chaotic din was maddening to his ears. The infected incessantly howled and chattered, screamed and cursed, murmured and mumbled.

Sometimes coherently.

Most times, the ravings of lunatics.

But he had to be there, for there had been incidents.

Escape attempts.

Hunters injured and killed.

He had to make certain that things didn't get out of hand. He had to protect his men as best he could. So he endured.

Guard duty.

That's what it was, pure and simple.

Imagine that.

How low he'd sunk, the great man. Once an arkon of the lord. One of the grand marshals of Azathoth — he who called himself the one true god. In those olden days, Azrael the Wise stood as a giant amongst men. He strode across Midgaard for years beyond count, doing deeds outside the ken of common folk.

Until one day, it all ended.

And the world turned on its head. That day he became a rebel. Some would say a traitor.

In later days, a crusader.

And when those great deeds were done, he became naught but a hermitish alchemist, doomed to spend eternity searching for a cure to the most lethal scourge ever known. A cure that might never be found.

Now, in these latter days, what was he?

A lowly dungeon guard.

Who would believe it?

What would Thetan say if he could see him now?

What would Mithron say?

How Uriel would laugh and poke fun at him.

Would they lose all respect for him? Worse, would they pity him?

And to think, he'd brought it all upon himself.

Two infected women in the cell to Azrael's right stared at him, coy smirks on their faces. He figured they were up to something. But maybe they just thought he was pretty. The women usually did.

Their stares made him uncomfortable, nervous. He felt his face flush. He felt the sweat bead on his brow. But he was flattered all the same. He tried not to stare back, but found that difficult — though not as difficult as being stared at.

Physically, both women appeared perfectly normal, save for a paleness of skin. Their garments were bloodstained. Stout iron collars affixed about their necks chained them to the wall. They couldn't reach within two feet of the bars on any side, and thus posed no threat at all.

Azrael knew that like all the infected, they could change their appearance at will. One moment they'd look perfectly normal, same as anyone, and the next, they'd transform, nearly instantly, into ravenous monsters of gray skin, black eyes, long fangs and claws. And but a moment later, they could turn human again, though they were loath to do so until they had fed to their fill. That power made it easy for the infected to walk amongst healthy folk and prey upon them. Azrael knew of no other disease remotely like it.

Both women were beautiful. Or at least pretty in their way, or so Azrael thought. He didn't get out much.

"These clothes are filthy," said one woman, a blonde, probably less than twenty, as she looked down at her shirt in disgust.

"I can't stand them," said the other girl, a few years older, dark-haired, and plump. "I'm taking them off. I won't wear these rags another moment."

They both slowly removed their garments, staring at Azrael all the while, seductive looks on their faces. They stripped to their undergarments, which were nearly as soiled.

It had been a long time since Azrael had seen a woman unclothed.

Years.

Too many years.

He found it strangely difficult to look away, so he didn't. Why should he?

The women moved close together and began to caress each other's bodies. Then they kissed. Tentatively, teasingly, at first. Then passionately. And at length. At every opportunity, they stared at Azrael as they put on their performance. Soon they were naked, entwined together. "Join us, Master," said one.

"Join us," said the other.

That was their game. An escape attempt. How big a fool did they think he was?

Things had gone quiet behind Azrael. He looked over his shoulder. The workmen had halted their labors. They all stood staring at the women, their expressions ran from lustful, to disgusted, to embarrassed, to angry.

Azrael turned back toward the women, and strangely, he stood before the cell door, several feet closer to the women than he had been a moment before. How he got there, he didn't know. But it was a better view.

Closer.

And that was good. Now he saw that their faces were beautiful. Flawless. Their curves, much curvier than he'd first thought. He wanted to be closer to them.

He needed to be.

18

THE DEAD FENS, THE KEEP

Year 1242, 4th Age
12th Year of King Tenzivel's Rule

The falling gate had pulverized the masonry at the edge of the stairwell opening and sent debris cascading down all about the Lomerians, battering and bruising them, and clouding their vision. Dust filled the stairwell's air so thickly that they could barely see or breathe, coughing and gagging. They retreated down the steps; first one landing down and then another to escape it.

"We can't leave Gabriel up there alone," said McDuff.

"The way is blocked off," said Malvegil, "and we can't clear it if the dust suffocates us. For a minute or two, he's on his own."

"The priest is out," said Karktan. "Fallen unconscious."

"You, Talbon, and Artol get him down to the bottom," shouted Aradon. "Wake him up if you can; make certain he's breathing, then get your tails back up here."

***

"**A**re you okay?" shouted someone, their voice familiar.

Brother Donnelin's eyelids fluttered as he regained consciousness. Somehow, despite the pain from his wounds, he had drifted off to sleep. And someone was waking him up. How nice.

Par Talbon fronted him and shook him by the shoulder, concern on his face.

"Aye, I'm okay," spat Donnelin through gritted teeth, though that wasn't the truth. Every inch of him hurt, and he was dead drunk.

"Stay here," said Talbon. "We'll be back. Don't try to follow." The wizard turned and ran up the steps, following the others who were already on their way up, weapons bared.

Donnelin looked down at his arm, hoping. Hoping it had been a nightmare. Hoping that his arm would still be there. Whole and sound.

It wasn't.

But that was no surprise; not really. He knew before he looked; the smell of burnt flesh hung heavy in the air. He knew why. Still, he cringed when his eyes locked on the bloody stump, heavily bandaged as it was. This was far worse than any nightmare could ever be.

At least he was still alive.

He wished Talbon hadn't woken him. It hurt less when he was asleep. He wanted to sleep until it stopped hurting. He wasn't certain how long he had been unconscious, and looked around to try to get his bearings.

He was at the base of a stairwell. Stone walls. Stone steps. Flaking paint. A lot of dust hanging in the air. Dim light from an oil-burning wall sconce. A door off to his left. It looked like the same stairwell they had gone up a little while ago, but he wasn't certain. Everything was a bit foggy. Okay, a lot foggy.

Moaning and howling came from behind the door. The shamblers! They were there. On the other side of the door. Then he remembered the laboratory, with all those shamblers pinned down or trussed up. Some madman must have been experimenting on them, or else torturing them. While they were in there, Donnelin desperately wanted to appropriate some of the tools and gadgets lying around. Ever the tinker was he. Tinkering was his passion, near as much as the old religion was. But he didn't have the strength. It was all he could do to keep his eyes open. No doubt, Talbon liberated a few things he'd get to examine later. And McDuff was probably so weighed down with "loot" that he could barely walk. The dwarf was a bit secretive and probably wouldn't even let him see the stuff. Probably best to not even ask him about it, and save himself the disappointment.

Donnelin looked up the stair, whence Talbon had gone. It must lead farther up into the keep. Into the high tower.

Something had happened up there that sent the others running up. More Lugron, or more shamblers, or maybe something worse. Odin knows what other horrors lurked within that keep. He half remembered a great shaking and crashing, but he wasn't certain whether it had been real or only a dream.

Donnelin had no interest in staying behind on his own. Especially not with a horde of shamblers in the next room, tied down or not. He pulled himself to his feet, his head swimming. He felt dizzy each time he turned his head, however slightly. He had tunnel vision, and even that was blurry. Was it the rum, or the blood loss, or the first effects of the disease creeping up on him? Maybe they hadn't caught it in time. Maybe he'd had his arm cut off for nothing. Maybe he was going to die anyway. To turn into an inhuman monster, like did poor Master Gorlick.

He didn't want to think about that. He couldn't. Better to die in battle. To end it quickly. Best he follow the others to achieve that end. So he started up the stairs, his legs shaky. Each step was a battle. He was so tired. So disoriented.

He made it up but a few steps before he gave up. He was simply too weak and far too drunk to be of any use to anyone. At least the alcohol made the pain of his lost arm bearable, if barely. Even still, that wound hurt worse than anything he'd felt before. He turned around, intending to take a seat on the steps. To rest for a few minutes. Maybe he'd even fall asleep again. Maybe he'd regain a bit of strength.

That's when he heard them.

Lugron.

In the laboratory. More than a few. It sounded as if they were headed toward the stairwell. The lock on the door was broken, no doubt from when the Lomerians entered. There was no crossbar. No way to secure the door.

He felt the adrenaline rush through his body. With newfound energy, he rushed up the steps to the first landing — about ten steps up. He looked up the spiral stair. Its top was a long, long way up. Beyond his sight, given the dim lighting in the place. There was no hope to make it even halfway there before the Lugron caught him. Not in his condition. The only choice that remained was to turn and fight.

He pulled out his dagger, prepared his magics, and stood ready to bar the Lugrons' path.

A warrior's death it would be.

That put a smile on his face.

19

THE HOLLOW, VIRENT HALL

Year 801, 4th Age

"**S**end them away, Master, and join us," said the blonde infected woman to Azrael as she beckoned him toward her with her fingers, her body still intimately intertwined with her lovely companion.

"We want you."

"We need you."

"Join us, now."

"We will make you happy."

"You belong with us."

Azrael turned the key in the cell's lock, though he knew not how the key ended up in his hand. Men shouted behind him. They urged him to stop. Why should he? One of the women had the largest breasts he'd ever seen. The other, nearly so. And they were perfect, the both of them. Their perfume exquisite, alluring. Their hair, lustrous. Their skin flawless. What man could resist them? And why should he?

The workmen moved closer, the bastards, shouting all the while. Who were they to tell him what to do? He was master here. He was the lord's Arkon, Azrael. Azrael the Wise.

And who were they?

Nothing.

Peasants.

Commoners.

Sell-swords.

"Stop," shouted the blonde. She stood as close to the bars as the chain permitted and looked toward the men. "Patience, boys," she said, her arm extended in their direction, her eyes locked on them, her hips wiggling back and forth. "You'll all get your turn. Every one of you. Just wait there, quietly, and you'll get all that you desire. All that you deserve."

Azrael wanted to look over his shoulder and see what the men were doing. To know which of them dared move to stop him. He'd thrash them for it. The traitors. They'd delayed his entry into the cell. They'd kept him from his women. Worse, they'd made the blonde angry. That wouldn't do. He needed her happy — them both happy. Then, they'd both make him happy. And that's what he deserved. They were all that he desired. All that he ever wanted. Nothing would keep him from them.

"Join us, my love," said the brunette.

They didn't need to ask him again. Azrael planned to have his way with both of them. More than once.

And there would be no "turns" for the other men. He'd banish them all, the traitors. Send them scurrying from the manor, their tails between their legs. Kill them if he had to. If they defied him or got in his way again. These women were his. And his alone. Or rather, he was theirs. Not that it mattered. No one would come between them. Not now. Not ever. Not again.

As Azrael stepped through the cell door toward his loves, the cord from which his ankh hung somehow caught on the door's lock. The moment he put his bare hand on the ankh to dislodge it, he was himself again, as if suddenly woken from a deep sleep.

He staggered back.

Nearly fell.

"You must join us now," said the brunette, her voice sharp, urgent. "We'll die without you. We need you now!"

Azrael's mind was in a fog; the last minutes blurry. The work crew stood frozen, mesmerized, every man staring at the blonde. The dirty, ragged blonde, too skinny for Azrael's taste. They'd bewitched him. Him!

Azrael knew what he had to do.

He caught them by surprise.

His sword now in hand, he leaped toward them.

Slash, stab, slash, slash.

All his power and fury behind each blow.

In the end, he took their heads.

Both women.

He killed them.

Upon the women's death, the workmen fell to the floor, dazed, groggy, but free of the women's thrall.

The other infected roared. They cursed and spat and threatened. They shook the bars of their cells. They pounded on the walls. They swore vengeance.

One of the workmen, the town cobbler, staggered toward the women's cell, moaning, tears in his eyes. Azrael didn't know what to do. Was he still under the infecteds' control? How could that be, they were dead? Was it one of the others? Could they all control men's minds? Should he cut the man down?

Before he decided, the man passed him by and staggered into the cell in a daze. Tears streaming down his face, he dropped down beside the brunette, her severed head two feet from her body, blood pooling. The cobbler called her name. Said he was sorry. Begged her not to leave him.

Only at that moment did Azrael remember. The brunette was his wife. And Azrael had killed her right before his eyes.

The weight of his mistake crashed down on him. He didn't need to kill the women. He had escaped their spell, and they were still chained. Of limited threat. He could have found another way. Gagged them, or blindfolded them, or something. But he didn't even try. He didn't kill them out of need. He killed them in anger.

In rage.

Why?

Because they bested him.

If only for a few moments, but they'd bested him. Bested the great Azrael. If not for chance and his ankh, he might well be dead or else, infected himself. All that he was, all that he'd endured, all that his work meant for Midgaard, nearly snuffed out, just like that. Those thoughts fueled his rage. And so he killed those women without mercy.

The cobbler looked up at Azrael.

Azrael expected to see hatred in his eyes. He expected the man to rage at him. Maybe even to come at him, fist or blade. To seek vengeance. But there was no anger on the cobbler's face.

There was only the shock of betrayal.

The man had trusted Azrael. Trusted him to keep his wife safe. And eventually, to cure her. To protect her.

Instead, he killed her.

Murdered her.

As if she was nothing.

No one.

Worthless.

Azrael hadn't even remembered she was his wife.

Why not? He knew her. He'd met them before all this, in their shop, more than once. That's where they captured her. The cobbler led them there.

Azrael had forgotten. He'd just forgotten.

People.

They were so ephemeral to Azrael. Their lives so short, so fleeting. So small. So unimportant.

Yet they were all important.

All important.

Their well-being was the very purpose of Azrael's life. Had he forgotten that? Had he lost sight of that? Had he lost his perspective?

He'd grown too old. Too distant. Too uncaring. Too much the mad old hermit. There might not be any going back from that.

"I'm sorry," said Azrael. In half a moment, he thought of several justifications for his actions. Several reasons and excuses that he could spout

114

out for the inexcusable; things that he could say that might lessen the sting of his crime.

Lessen his guilt.

But then, he thought better of it. He kept those excuses inside. He pushed them down. He hated himself for even conjuring them up. Azrael was not a man to run from his mistakes, to shirk his responsibilities.

He had failed the cobbler and his wife.

He failed The Hollow.

He failed all of Midgaard.

"I am so sorry," he said.

And that was all he said.

And it was the truth.

The cobbler nodded. And he wept.

"We should kill them all," whispered one of the blacksmiths to Azrael. "If they can control our minds, it's only a matter of time before they get loose and kill us or infect us."

"There's been enough killing," said Azrael. "Instead, we'll take better precautions. We won't let this happen again."

It took a full day, night, and half the next day, and cost the lives of two men, but Azrael and the hunters bound the hands of all the imprisoned infected behind their backs, placed gags in their mouths, and covered their eyes with blindfolds. There would be no more trickery. No more spells. No more mind control. To be certain, Azrael placed the ankh under his shirt, resting against his bare skin, where its power was strongest. He knew not the nature of the magic that the infected harbored, but he was confident that the ankh would hold it at bay.

***

"Should I tell the hunters?" said Azrael. "That I created it? The contagion. The bloodlust."

"You did not create the contagion, Master," said Refisal. "You created a cure. A flawed one. But a cure was all you strove for. Your motivations were pure."

"There's no need to humor me," said Azrael. "We both know full well that the serum was meant only to cure, not harm anyone. That doesn't change the fact that it did harm them. That it was the source of this plague. So I ask you again, should I tell them?"

"To what end?" said Refisal.

"It would ease my conscience if they knew the truth. If I could make them understand."

"You seek forgiveness?" said Refisal.

"I don't want to live a lie."

"If you tell them, you won't live at all," said Refisal. "They'll kill you."

"You don't think I could make them understand?"

"I doubt you'd have the chance to try."

Azrael nodded. "You may be right. At least you know the truth."

"And I don't blame you," said Refisal.

"I blame myself," said Azrael.

"I know."

20

THE DEAD FENS, THE KEEP

Year 1242, 4th Age
12th Year of King Tenzivel's Rule

So long had the two metal warriors been but statues, as they awoke, they strained and struggled to flex their massive arms, rusted and stiff from disuse, age, and the elements. Their movements sent metal shards flying, the metallic screeching painful to hear. So too did they flex their fingers, opening and closing their fists, green and silver paint crumbling and flaking off, exposing rough red iron beneath. Then, with a great grinding of metal, they turned their heads in Gabriel's direction, sparks shooting from their necks, their eyes, black pits with glowing red pupils.

From far across the hall, they studied Gabriel with those soulless, vacant eyes, devoid of any semblance of humanity. They stepped forward, toward Gabriel, their legs stiff and slow, creaking and clattering as they went, each movement a battle as they shook off their slumber. Each ponderous step produced an echoey, hollow thump. A strange mechanical hum was in the air — a whirling and a buzzing, its origin and purpose unknown save that it came from the metallic men.

"Golems," spat Gabriel as he eyed the metal men and shook his head. He hadn't seen one of their kind in more years than he could remember. No expert on them was he, but he knew some little of their lore. Often, golems were magical constructs — some strange spark of life imbued in them by a sorcerer or archmage of sufficient knowledge and power to tap the grand weave of magic in just the right manner.

For reasons unknown to Gabriel, golem creation was considered a dark art, the procedure shunned by wizards of nobler purpose and proper social standing, or so it was said. That made those golems that were born of sorcery (and their creators), things best avoided by folk of goodly nature.

Other golems were born of grand metalcraft by tinkers of singular skill. Those golems were machines. Things of science, not sorcery. Powered either by the burning of one fuel or another, or by use of strange crystals extracted from the bowels of Midgaard or fallen from the heavens.

The creation of either type of golem, magic or machine, was a lost art — even the great archmages of Lomion City's Tower of the Arcane, and the master artisans of the Tinkers Guild, possessed not the knowledge. At least, they did no longer. As far as Gabriel was concerned, that was a good thing for Midgaard, for although they were useful guardians, golems were terrible foes — mindless and merciless in pursuit of whatever was their mission, fair or foul. They couldn't be reasoned with or tricked. They couldn't be bargained with, bribed, or intimidated. They never got tired or hungry or sick. And worse, they never gave up. Not ever.

How Azrael came to possess two such things, Gabriel couldn't imagine. He doubted that he'd created them himself — he was no metal worker and his delvings into magic, though deep and broad, did not venture much toward the dark arts.

Not in the past, at least.

But of old, neither did they venture toward necromancy — a dark art to which Azrael had since become expert, it seemed.

The first golem lumbered toward Gabriel, picking up speed and agility with each stride. The second golem had only moved a step or two, its legs more rusted than its fellow's, its joints stiff and unresponsive. It strained against itself, struggling to take a step, but its legs couldn't comply. It stumbled, lost its balance, and crashed down with a thunderous thud. Its corroded knee joint shattered on impact and pulverized the stone flooring beneath it. The whole room shook with that impact, the floor slab threatening to give way unto the floor below. The golem toppled over, its leg a ruin, fully broken off at the knee. It thrashed about, confused and unable to rise.

Gabriel was at the bars by the stairwell. A glance confirmed that the stairs weren't completely blocked though they were covered in debris. The dust hung thick in the air; his comrades, out of sight. They must have retreated down farther to escape the choking cloud. So for the moment, he was on his own.

The bars were thick and solid. Given time, he'd get through them — either by his own devices or with help from the others. But there was no time. The lead golem would soon be on him. He had but a few moments.

He heaved up on the bars with all his power but the iron did not budge. He knew at once that the bars were connected to some geared mechanism hidden up above the ceiling. No force could lift them until that mechanism was disengaged or broken. His eyes raced over the bars, searching for a weak point — somewhere that corrosion had taken its toll. Some defect that he could exploit. But in those few moments, he found nothing.

And then the golem's fist crashed down.

21

THE HOLLOW, FALSTAD MANOR

Year 801, 4th Age

As usual, it was the stench that caught Azrael first. The overwhelming reek of rotting flesh, the smell of death, so potent that he wanted to vomit. He caught the first whiff of it as he and his hunters crept up the lane, still a hundred yards from Falstad Manor. That one whiff was enough to turn less determined men about.

But not Azrael.

And not his hunters.

They'd weathered unspeakable horrors during the past weeks. It had hardened them. Changed them.

Old as he was, it even changed Azrael. His once immaculate armor was stained and soiled to ruin, blood and gore dried on it — that of the infected that could not be taken alive. He'd given up cleaning it, the armor. He'd never done that before. For all his years, he'd treated his martial equipment as his most prized possessions. He never neglected them. Their value, part practical (their use for defense) and part sentimental. Unlike most objects that a man can own or possess, metal (well-cared for) can last a very long time. His armor and weapons were old friends that had weathered war and strife with him. They connected him to his past in a way that otherwise, only the ankh and his memories did. That made them valuable to him. And so he cherished them.

Suddenly, that changed. At first, he told himself that he didn't have the time to clean and upkeep them; that there were more important things to worry about. Higher priorities.

But that wasn't it.

He just didn't care anymore. He just didn't feel like himself anymore. The guilt weighed heavily on him.

It was all his fault. All the death, the horror, the madness. It was all his fault.

The front door ajar, the stench hit them harder on the porch. But inside Falstad Manor, the stench was so much worse.

There are no words to describe it.

Azrael and the hunters bore it owing only to the wet cloths that they wrapped around their mouths and noses to dull it, and the treant leaf resin and peppermint leaves that they smeared across their upper lips to mask it. But nothing eliminated it; not that stench. Their clothes would stink of it until thoroughly washed, if even then. Their hair too. Even their skin, as if the very pores absorbed the odor. Even their excrement would stink of it.

They moved cautiously as they spread out into the foyer of Falstad Manor for the fourth time since the night of Pennebray's party. The first three times they'd come up empty. No infected were found. Only the dead.

But Azrael knew that Lady Dahlia and Pennebray had come back to that place. And it wasn't only because most of the infected returned to their homes or other places they had frequented. He sensed them. He couldn't say how exactly, but he detected their presence in the manor. He knew that they lurked somewhere within. Hiding. It was a huge place. Even larger than Virent Hall. It might prove no easy task to root them out.

No doubt, the ankh was behind it, the sensing of them. That ancient talisman had ever been skilled at wayfinding. It guided Azrael when he needed guiding, even when he didn't call on its aid. Simply wearing it about his neck, as he'd always done, evoked its power, and its aid, however subtly. That relic was his good right hand and it had rarely let him down.

They'd scoured the town, Azrael and his hunters did.

Every building.

Every basement.

Every barn and root cellar.

Every crypt on Ancestor Hill.

They'd rooted them out, the infected.

Hundreds of them.

They'd multiplied so quickly. As many as there were, there could have been more. Far more. But rather than infect most of their victims, they killed them outright.

Then they ate them.

Parts of them at least. If they had time, if they weren't interrupted, they'd eat them to the bone, leaving next to nothing behind. It seemed that they couldn't help themselves. The smell of blood drove them to a killing frenzy. The sight of it banished all reason and judgment from their minds. It left them as rabid dogs — wild, ravenous, mindless killers. They'd stalk and kill anyone, without mercy or conscience.

Friends.

Loved ones.

Family.

Even their own children.

Yet between feedings, they could blend in. They could look and behave normally. Oh how deadly that made them.

Nothing satiated their bloodlust, save for engorgement, a state akin to overeating taken to morbid extremes. The infected could consume tens of pounds of raw flesh and huge quantities of blood — and did so whenever the opportunity presented. They couldn't help themselves. They couldn't stop. They ate until they could barely move. Until they nearly burst. And that was their weakness. That was when they were most vulnerable.

Those few victims of the infected that escaped death soon joined their ranks. And when they turned, however strong or pious their former character, the bloodlust took over and they became as monsters.

Sometimes it was only a matter of hours before they turned. Other times, a day, maybe two, if the wound were small and their constitution strong. But all that were bitten succumbed to their fate. They were doomed.

Every one. No matter their strength. No matter their resolve.

Once turned, they were hardly encumbered by the wounds and blood loss inflicted by the infected that had attacked them, however terrible their nature and extent. Most of their injuries were quick to heal and often disappeared entirely; not even a scar left behind.

22

THE DEAD FENS, INSIDE THE KEEP

Year 1242, 4th Age
12th Year of King Tenzivel's Rule

One moment Gabriel was there by the bars, the golem's fist aimed for his head; the next, he'd tumbled out of the way faster than a skilled acrobat. The golem's fist struck the bars a glancing blow — the sound akin to a dull bell being rung.

Gabriel fled through the hall, searching for other exits and any weapon he could use along the way; his sword and daggers were in their sheathes — useless against solid metal. The small battle hammer he wore at his belt would be nearly as useless.

The golem pursued him, its speed impressive. All its will and purpose set on destroying Gabriel. Whatever password Gabriel failed to guess or lever he failed to pull, had set the golem on its quest against him. It marked him as an intruder. An intruder that must die.

Gabriel knew that the golem would not rest until its deed was done, however long it took, whether but a moment or a hundred years. It would pursue him. And not just throughout this single hall, not just throughout the keep.

126

It would follow him out into the Fens.

And beyond. Far beyond.

Unto the very ends of Midgaard if need be. Over land or sea, mountain or desert, relentless and unyielding, until its task was accomplished or its weird spark of life failed, and it returned to a lifeless heap of metal. Such was its nature.

The golem thundered forward, its heavy steps shaking the tower to its roots. It made no effort to go around any obstacle, but rather went through them, crushing and splintering couches, chairs, and anything else between it and its prey.

As Gabriel raced around the room, at last, he saw what he needed. Hung on the far wall, off to the side of the great throne, an array of weapons and shields adorned the wall, long enshrouded in a thick layer of dust and soot. There hung bladed weapons of ornate and exotic make: swords and a collection of daggers, bejeweled and honed to a razor's edge; spears and halberds, axes, and maces.

But what caught his eye was a massive battle hammer, long hafted and flat headed. That hammer was layered with years of dust and grime, but it would serve.

Gabriel snatched it from the wall. A weighty thing it was, even for him. Far too heavy for any common man to wield in battle. The hammer's head, a massive thing of solid steel; its haft, a thick wooden pole — so old, so hard, it felt more stone than wood. Weapons of its size and weight were not made anymore. And rare was the weapon so ornately inscribed with the old runic script, head and haft alike. It was a relic: a holdover from the days of yore, from the Age of Myth and Legend, that time before the great plague. Battered and scarred, a veteran of long wars and countless years, it had been wielded by men of power, but of their names, their deeds, no one would ever know, save perhaps Azrael, if even he possessed the knowledge. And if he still lived.

Gabriel never favored a big hammer for battle. A clumsy, slow weapon. He preferred the sword, or even an axe. Yet against a golem, perhaps there was nothing better.

Just after Gabriel plucked the hammer from its perch, the golem's iron fist barreled in, aimed for his head.

Gabriel ducked.

The heavy masonry wall exploded above him from the thunderous impact of that punch; windows broke high up in the wall from the vibration, and masonry and glass rained down on Gabriel as he shielded his head as best he could.

Gabriel dashed toward the throne, the golem in hot pursuit, then bounded atop the throne's steps in a single leap. Two more quick steps took him to the throne's seat, then its armrest. In a single motion did Gabriel do this, neither pausing nor slowing. Glancing back at the golem, he turned his body and leaped down, swinging the hammer in a mighty overhead arc as he went. The golem reacted, but was too slow to dodge or parry the attack, if even it was capable of such actions.

The hammer struck the golem in the head — a perfect hit, all Gabriel's power behind it — a blow that would have killed most any living creature.

Gabriel expected its head to shatter. He expected the golem to collapse lifeless to the floor.

It didn't.

Gabriel landed hard. The hammer, lost. His arms half numb; all strength gone from his hands.

The golem's foot stamped down toward his head. The thing wasn't even fazed. Gabriel rolled aside, the merest moment away from being crushed to pulp. He made his feet. He needed a moment to get his bearings, and solid cover to hold the golem back, if need be. He sprinted across the hall, looking for any spot of refuge, however temporary.

The golem lumbered after him. It didn't look injured. The hammer had barely left a mark — the golem's head, not the hollow shell he expected, but a solid block of forged iron. His mightiest blow did no more damage to it, than would a hammer to an anvil.

He knew not how to stop the thing.

He wasn't certain whether anything could.

Worse, as best he could tell, there was no way out of the hall save for the blocked stairwell. He was trapped, good and proper.

23

THE HOLLOW, FALSTAD MANOR

Year 801, 4th Age

During the first few nights after Pennebray's party, while the engorged infected wallowed like snakes, after their slaughter of the townsfolk, Azrael hunted them down.

He and his hunters marched from house to house and sought them out, captured all those they could, and killed the rest. At first, finding them was easy enough, for most of the infected slunk back to their homes to rest and recover from their feasting. Like nocturnal animals, they preferred to move about and hunt at night, shunning the midday sun.

So more often than not, during the day, they slept. And when engorged, their sleep was deep. So deep they could often be taken unawares. Those that woke, were sluggish and disoriented from their gluttony; easy prey for Azrael and the grim hunters that he gathered to his side. But some few were found awake and aware — so strong, so fast, so agile. Terrible, terrible foes that fought without mercy. Swift and violent went those battles.

Many hunters died in those first bloody days. But their sacrifice and Azrael's leadership slowed the spread of the bloodlust, the bulk of the infected rounded up or killed in the space of but three or four days.

And that was all that saved Midgaard.

When Azrael's work in the town proper was done, he expanded his hunting range to the outlying farms in all directions. Those places nearest to town were invariably deserted; their inhabitants killed or gone missing. Some farms were devoid of man and beast. Others were populated by one or more of the infected who feasted on the farm's bounty, human and animal alike.

Azrael dealt with them, one and all.

Those farms farther afield were mostly unscathed, thank the gods. A few isolated souls were still oblivious of what went on and thought the hunters mad when they approached them and warned of blood-sucking cannibals.

Azrael and his men followed what trails they found, and tracked the infected down wherever they went. Multiple days went by in which Azrael didn't sleep. He rode horses to the ground as he flew from one farm to the next and the next and the next. What hunters that were capable of following, did so. Sometimes, Azrael went in alone. He wouldn't rest until it was done. He was loath to kill the infected, despite their terrible deeds; despite the monsters that they'd become, though far more often than not, kill them he had to, or else they would have killed him.

He so wanted to cure them. He needed to. He couldn't be the cause, however unintentionally, of so many deaths.

Not again.

He couldn't bear it again.

After weeks of blood and horror, eventually, the task was done.

Azrael had won.

There were no more infected to be found. All were dead, or imprisoned in Azrael's dungeon. But there were at least two infected that remained missing. Azrael had to find them. He could not let even one get away, no matter the cost. For one could spread the contagion to many. Let loose in one of the big cities, the disease would be unstoppable.

As best as Azrael could tell, Lady Dahlia and Pennebray were the last. They were the only infected folk that were for certain unaccounted for. But Azrael couldn't be sure that no others remained at large, for so many victims of the slaughter were never identified — either too little was left of them, or no one alive knew who they were. And more than a few folk had gone missing without a trace.

Azrael tracked the last few infected by their deeds — by the trail of attacks, death, destruction that they left in their wake. Were there some out there that were smart enough to cover their tracks; to evade the hunters? To hide? Were there some that had run off, far from The Hollow? That had escaped them? Azrael didn't know. And that troubled him. So much so that he could barely speak of it. It haunted him; the guilt, the fear of it, the dread. The fear that this plague that he'd unwittingly unleashed would spread like wildfire and devour the world. The weight of that was too much for any man to bear. It kept him awake most nights, all night. He grew short of temper, his judgment faltered. He barely ate.

Before arriving at House Falstad that day, Azrael's hunters had found not a single infected for a full week. While the hunters hunted, Azrael spent much of that week locked in his laboratory with Refisal as they frantically searched for a cure. During that time, there were no new attacks. Not one. What goodly folks remained in town, hunkered down in groups. Many at Virent Hall, most of the rest at the Odinhome and the schoolhouse. There was safety in numbers.

And Azrael wouldn't let them leave. He set up roadblocks on every road, lane, path, and trail that led out of town. Townsfolk and mercenaries (that Azrael paid handsomely) manned the roadblocks.

He had to keep The Hollow isolated.

He couldn't take the chance that someone would spread the contagion across the countryside.

Azrael knew that Lady Dahlia and Pennebray couldn't stay hidden forever. The disease drove them to eat meat and drink blood, and for that they needed victims, though it seemed that animals served as well as people, for they'd found the ravaged remains of many house pets and livestock during their hunts.

But how strong was that drive to feed? And how necessary? Azrael didn't know. The data was confusing, inconsistent. And he had no time to conduct a proper study.

Those infected that he held in the manor's dungeon didn't seem to need to eat at all. He had the servants prepare food for them every day, just as if they were welcome house guests. Some of them ate the food without issue or complaint. Most threw it back at the servants. Some threw it up, vomiting at the mere touch of bread, fruit, or vegetables to their lips.

They only wanted meat.

And preferred it raw or nearly so. They wanted it bloody. The bloodier the better.

But those that didn't eat at all, seemed little the worse for it. Angrier, more bestial was their behavior, but they didn't grow weak or sickly. They endured.

Since there were no new attacks on people or animals in town, that meant and infecteds at large were going hungry (in which case they could be hold up anywhere) or else, they were feeding on the dead. The one place in town that had more dead bodies than anywhere else was Falstad Manor, owing to the massacre during Pennebray's party.

Azrael hadn't burned the manor down, though several of the hunters had urged him to do so. He'd found that since the infected so often returned to their homes, the best way to catch them was to await them there. So Falstad Manor still stood, despite the gruesome slaughter that had occurred within.

24

THE DEAD FENS, THE KEEP

Year 1242, 4th Age
12th Year of King Tenzivel's Rule

Gabriel heard a commotion from far across the hall, back by the stair. McDuff and Artol were at the bars. They pounded them over and again with their hammers, trying to break their way through. The other Lomerians were with them. Gabriel was happy for the help, and impressed anew by their bravery and loyalty, since most men would flee from what he was fighting, not seek to meet it. But what could they do against a creature like the golem? It may well be the death of them all.

The need to escape consumed Gabriel's thoughts. Perhaps he need not fight the thing at all. If the others got the bars bent just enough for him to slip through, they could get away and the golem might be contained. He knew that his friends would make a breach somehow. He was certain of it. Once outside, and out of immediate danger, he'd figure out a way to put the golem down, even if he had to bring the whole keep down atop it.

He had to destroy it. He couldn't let the golem be since there was no way to call it off. No way to shut it down. He needed to buy some time. Time for the others to do their work on the bars. Evasion was the logical choice, but he'd not run around the hall like a scared chicken.

That was not his way.

True to his nature, Gabriel turned and went straight at the golem, hammer swinging.

The golem was surprisingly agile, despite its bulk, but Gabriel was far the quicker. He ducked a roundhouse punch and slammed the hammer into the golem's knee. So hard was that blow, so unyielding was that iron knee, that Gabriel nearly dropped the hammer again, his hands and forearms trembling. He ignored the pain and lost not a moment before attacking again. He spun around and slammed the hammer to the backside of the same knee.

That powerful strike buckled its knee and overbalanced the golem. It fell backwards, flat on its back. The room shook with the thunderous impact, the sound of stone and glass cracking and falling filled the air. For a moment, Gabriel wondered whether the whole tower was about to collapse. Gabriel raised the hammer overhead with both hands, poised to slam it down on the golem's face.

This time, the golem was too quick. It dodged its head to the side, the blow missing it by a hair's breadth, the hammer's head blasting into the stone slab.

Gabriel's hammer crashed into the golem's jaw as it tried to stand — a powerful blow that drove the golem's head back. Gabriel spun in a tight arc and whipped the hammer's head against the thing's other cheek. Then he lifted the great hammer overhead to bring it down atop the golem's head.

But that blow never landed.

The golem's hand shot out and grabbed Gabriel under the armpit. It effortlessly lifted him up, Gabriel, struggling, but effectively helpless. He could not slip its grip. He thought he was done for. He thought the thing was about to pull him apart. But instead, it threw him at the nearest wall.

That wall was twenty feet away.

He hit it hard.

Very hard.

Some men, perhaps most, would have died then and there, the impact hard enough to shatter half their bones and crush any number of internal organs. But alive or dead, they'd be helpless, or nearly so, and out of the fight.

Gabriel was no common man.

He found himself in a sitting position, his back against the wall, all the wind knocked out of him, his strength sapped, his head spinning. But he was alive. In one piece. And as best he could tell, not grievously injured.

It was then that he felt, as much as heard, a powerful blast of eldritch energy. Within moments, the scent of molten metal filled the air. It could only mean one thing: Par Talbon had blasted through the gates! Help was on the way. And now there was a way out.

Gabriel raised his chin and looked up at the golem that approached him. The thing wasn't done with him.

It had no mercy.

It wouldn't stop until he was nothing but a pile of gore and a bloody stain on the floor.

In two strides, the thing was in an all-out charge. Untold thousands of pounds of iron barreled toward Gabriel — an unstoppable juggernaut intent upon crushing him to pulp. Its steps were like thunder. The whole hall shook. The entire tower shook.

Gabriel rose to his haunches despite his spinning head. At the last moment before the golem crashed into him, he sprang aside. How he accomplished that, shaken as he was, he could never say.

The golem didn't stop.

It didn't even try. It crashed headlong into the stone wall — and kept going, the wall exploding into untold fragments from its impact.

More masonry crashed down as the upper portion of the wall collapsed. Glass rained down from on-high. Dust billowed up obscuring everything.

Gabriel struggled to his feet, dizzy and bruised, covered in dust and debris, not certain how badly he was injured, if even at all. A fog of dust was about him, which made it hard to breathe. Blood dripped from here and there, his face and hands mostly, small cuts from glass shards or sharp stone fragments. His armor had well protected him from more serious injury.

Then it grabbed his leg.

Gabriel didn't see it coming, the dust so thick. He didn't know it was there until it grabbed him. Not the golem he'd been fighting. That one was somewhere on the other side of the collapsed wall. The one that grabbed him was the other one — old One Leg. It lay prone on the floor, but its grip was iron like its body. It clamped down on Gabriel's leg and wouldn't let go.

The battle hammer lay between Gabriel and the golem, though off to the side by a ways. No easy reach. Gabriel tried for it, but fell inches short. He twisted and pulled.

Then the golem started to pull him closer.

Gabriel stretched to his limit, straining for every possible inch. Fingertips found the haft. Moments later, the hammer was in Gabriel's grasp.

He raised the weapon and swung it at the golem's wrist as best he could from a sitting position. The blow had no good affect, for the thing clamped down all the tighter on his leg, those iron fingers an immovable vice — so powerful were they, he knew his flesh would withstand them for but a few moments more before being crushed.

Gabriel twisted, trying to get a better angle and more leverage. He brought down the hammer again. It smashed into One Leg's arm. But it was no use. Gabriel couldn't get enough power behind his blows — the thing was too close, the weapon's haft too long, his movements too restricted. His blow jarred his own leg, and sent shooting pains all the way to his core.

One Leg clamped down all the harder on his ankle. It dragged him closer. Closer to its gaping maw filled of iron teeth. Why the thing needed teeth or a maw at all, Gabriel had no idea.

Gabriel wouldn't give up. He'd not be beaten by that thing. He'd find a way to destroy it. He hit it with the hammer again, and again, and again, like a carpenter pounding a nail.

It wasn't enough. He couldn't get his leg free. There was no escape.

And then McDuff was there, roaring dwarven battle cries, his great axe working up and down, going at the golem. Artol was a step behind him. He brought his hammer down on One Leg's head, all his vast strength behind it. The other Lomerians were all around, attacking One Leg with whatever weapons they had.

Aradon grasped Gabriel about the shoulders, Ob at his side. At some point during the pounding, One Leg finally released Gabriel, and Aradon immediately pulled him clear.

One Leg thrashed about, swiping at the men with its hands, kicking at them with its remaining foot. It tried to rise, or to make it to its knees, but the Lomerians pummeled it back down, over and again.

"The gate is down," said Aradon to Gabriel. "Can you walk? We've got to get out."

"Get me up," said Gabriel. The golem's grip had numbed his leg. It was barely responsive, shooting pains traveling up and down, toes to torso.

Aradon, Ob, and Gabriel moved to the breach in the wall (the one the other golem had crashed through) when they heard a great rumbling beyond the breach, outside on the terrace roof. Luck had favored them, for what they saw was almost a comical sight.

The terrace's structure had partially collapsed under the golem's massive weight — whatever beams once supported that roof, now broken or deflected beyond repair. A large swath of roof sloped toward the golem; stone pavers, the terrace's walking surface, had slid toward the golem and piled around it. The golem itself was trapped in a hole that had opened beneath its feet and swallowed its legs and most of its torso. And it was slipping.

"It's stuck," said Aradon. "And the other one can't walk. Let's get the others and be gone from here."

"We have to finish this," said Gabriel. "There's a magic in these things. They won't let us go. They'll follow us home."

"To the Dor?" said Aradon. "It's fifty leagues from here. They'll never make it through the bog. They'll never even know which way we went."

"They'll make it and they'll know," said Gabriel. "We have to stop them here and now. You two go help the others. Find a way to destroy the one-legged one. I'll deal with the one on the roof."

25

THE HOLLOW, FALSTAD MANOR

Year 801, 4th Age

Falstad Manor was dark, quiet, and seemingly deserted — exactly the same as it had been during each of their visits since that terrible, bloody night of Pennebray's party.

Bloodstains everywhere.

Rotting body parts littered the floor — not enough left to identify the victims. Some were nothing more than bones, gnawed upon, covered with teeth marks.

Furniture overturned and smashed.

The hunters crept into the grand foyer, weapons and nets in hand. They moved cautiously and stayed close together, moving back to back whenever possible. There were nine of them, counting Azrael and old Refisal. Those were all that were left of a force of more than a hundred fighting men. Many folk still manned the roadblocks, but each was too old, sickly, or injured to join the hunters.

The nine hunters soldiered on, each for their own reasons: revenge, coin, hope for a cure for their beloveds, or loyalty to Azrael. They stood by him through battle, blood, and death. Every man amongst them was battered, bruised, and

142

scarred, pushed to their limits. But they were tough, strong, determined. Azrael was proud to lead them. It had been so long since he'd led men to war.

Perhaps too long.

Azrael's face was forlorn, his cheeks sunken. He'd eaten little over the past weeks.

"There is no sign of them, Master," said Refisal, as they searched about the main floor. "The vapors here are—"

"They're here," said Azrael. "I can feel them. They were here the last time too, but they fled us. Each day that has gone by, they've grown stronger, quicker. They are growing into their newfound powers; getting bolder. All while we've grown weaker — killed or injured one by one. So few of us left, they will not flee us this time, I think. We've been lucky in containing the spread of the bloodlust thus far. Tonight, we need to put an end to it. Here and now."

"As you say, we are few now," said Refisal. "That puts us at great risk. If they are more powerful than they were, perhaps it's best that we steer clear of them until help arrives from the north."

"If we had waited for help, this disease would have spread far and wide by now," said Azrael. "The whole countryside would be awash in blood and death. Who knows how far it would have spread already. Can you imagine what would happen if this thing made it to one of the big cities? We're on our own in this, men."

"Aargh!" came a scream from behind.

Pennebray, or rather the thing that once was Pennebray, was at the mason's neck, perched on his back, hands to shoulders, biting and tearing, blood spurting into the air. Where she sprang from, none could say.

Azrael could hardly bear to look at her. The thought of that sweet, beautiful little girl turned into a flesh-eating monster — and all because of him — was too much to bear. Far better that she had died that night when her mother brought her to his door. Far better for her, her mother, and for all of Midgaard.

But Azrael couldn't let her die; not in his home, not under his watch.

Was it empathy for her and her mother that drove him to try the serum on her even though it was against his better judgment? Was it to gain the favor of her mother? A woman of great beauty.

Was it his pride? Or that he couldn't stand failure? Couldn't bear criticism? After all, what was his worth if he couldn't even save a suffering little girl? What kind of alchemist or wizard was he, if he couldn't even do that?

So he went reckless.

Foolhardy.

The arrogance of it. Experimenting on a child with an untested serum.

Unconscionable.

Criminal.

And the whole town paid the price for his poor judgment. The whole town.

They paid in blood.

They paid with their lives.

And if Azrael didn't stop her now, and any more like her still left at large, all of Midgaard would suffer for his foolishness.

The men spun and moved toward Pennebray. She bounded off the mason as he fell, a geyser of blood spouting from his neck. Pennebray disappeared into the shadows.

Then Azreal heard the growling. It came from all around, from the darkness beyond the limits of their light. It was not but one or two infected that they faced.

It was many!

The eyes. The glowing eyes in the dark. So many! It would be a hard fight. One that they might not win.

Azrael heard a flutter from above him, like that of a bird taking flight. As he glanced up, Lady Dahlia crashed down atop him, head and shoulders, a maniacal look on her face, having leapt down from the top of the grand stair, a fall of twenty feet.

THE DEAD FENS, THE KEEP

Year 1242, 4th Age
12th Year of King Tenzivel's Rule

While Gabriel fought the golem on the terrace, Aradon and the others surrounded old One Leg and pounded on it with whatever they had. Only McDuff went at it with a bladed weapon — his huge axe. How that weapon didn't shatter or break in two upon impact with solid iron, none of the others could fathom, though it was well known that all of McDuff's weapons were forged of an esoteric alloy held close by dwarven metalsmiths.

The Lomerians dodged and sidestepped One Leg's blows, the golem hampered by its lost limb. They hit it from all sides, then withdrew from its range each time it counterattacked. Even their concerted strikes had little affect — a minor dent here, a scratch there. Nothing more.

"Pass me your hammer," shouted Aradon to Artol. The great lord of the Eotrus stepped up, that massive hammer in hand, his thick arms bulging, and blasted One Leg's jaw with a devastating swing.

One Leg, who had been kneeling, unable to rise, fell backward in slow motion, overbalanced by the power of Aradon's strike. One Leg slammed to the floor; the entire hall vibrated, the floor bucking beneath the Lomerians' feet.

In but a moment, One Leg bounced up, back to its knees, its agility uncanny, seemingly unhurt save for an ugly dent across its face — the impression of the hammer's head forever emblazoned there.

McDuff's axe blasted across the back of the golem's neck — a blow of such power that it would've taken a bull's head off. The axe left its mark — a narrow slit across the thing's nape, but of almost no depth. The blow had no effect.

Aradon came in once more, and hit the golem in the head, once and then again, and again, even as Malvegil and the others pounded its limbs and torso.

But One Leg wouldn't go down.

The thing was unstoppable.

Par Talbon had little choice. All his reserves of strength and will had been used up in the battle outside the keep. He managed to take down the gates at the top of the stairs, melting and blasting the bars away with the last bit of strength he could muster. He had nothing left. Yet, he was needed again.

Such was the lot of a war wizard.

Talbon's face was gaunt and drawn, a grayish cast to it, more akin to the shamblers outside, than to his normal self. His arms shook, his hands too. His fingers felt afire. Red and burned were they. Blisters here and there about hands and arms, face and neck. He rarely suffered so from his sorcery. He'd rarely thrown so much powerful magic over so short a span. And now he was paying the price.

The pain from the magic he'd thrown was terrible; the cut across his belly, forgotten in its wake. Already he'd choked down what remedies he could: arrowroot leaf and cottonrounds — he'd been chewing on them since the battle outside. He even smeared oil of adarisk on his fingertips and the backs of his hands, and on the blisters wherever he found them. He hated the smell of that stuff, but had to stop the burning. And it wasn't even enough. Not nearly. He wanted to curl up into a ball and cry.

That was unlike him — not an emotional man was Par Talbon, not by a long stretch. When it came to his duties as a war wizard, he was icy cold, his will of iron. But the pain was too much for him to stoically bear. He could keep it neither from his face or his posture. He was hurting. And his friends knew it.

He could do no more to help. He'd done his part and then some.

But he was needed again.

If he threw more magic — not some petty cantrip or minor illusion, but something weighty, something of real power, in his present state, it might well kill him. He was that close to the edge. The others didn't know that. But he did.

His father, Par Mardack, would never abide him holding back, not when duty demanded or glory loomed. For the honor of House Montrose, he'd have him blast away, throwing caution to the wind, laughing in death's face.

The pompous ass.

The stinking blowhard.

No doubt, Mardack would soon be named a grandmaster of the Tower of the Arcane — his lifelong ambition. One that he prized above everything else, family included.

Talbon had no such ambitions, and no interest in the politics of the Tower, but his father's words, fair and foul, his encouragement, and his incessant criticism were never far from his mind.

He would not let down his liege lord, his comrades, or (grievances aside) his father — no matter the price fate demanded he pay.

He would do his duty even if it meant his death.

He didn't wait for a command from his liege. He said his mystic words, shouted for the others to stand clear, and let fly his sorcery.

A continuous beam of translucent light of reddish hue shot from the palm of his right hand, loudly humming and crackling as it went. The magical light sizzled and smoked upon impact with One Leg's shoulder, sparks flying about, raining on all and everything around.

The golem reeled from the terrible power of that sorcery. So strong was the light of that beam, that magic, that it superheated and melted solid iron in but mere moments.

Rivulets of molten metal dripped down from where the beam hit.

Talbon kept the beam trained on the creature, tracking its every movement, focusing the magic as best he could on the joint where the golem's arm met its shoulder and chest.

One Leg thrashed, and lashed out at the Lomerians, but they'd all stepped out of its range, fearful of getting caught up in Talbon's magic. Talbon tried to hold the beam steady on that shoulder joint, moving it along the seam — a challenging task with the golem thrashing about.

Within moments, the magic thoroughly melted and gouged the metal on both sides of the shoulder joint. That metal quickly cooled and hardened when Talbon pulled the beam away. As it hardened, the joint went stiff, just as Talbon planned. At first, the metal squealed and rent when One Leg moved its arm, but after some moments, the skirling sounds ground to a halt when the arm could move no more. It was locked into place by the distorted joint, never to move again.

Talbon refocused his heat ray on the joint between One Leg's thigh and its torso, the metal quickly melting and then cooling, rendering that joint as useless as the other.

Talbon fell to one knee. His hands smoked and blistered, worse than before, but he kept his spell going, and poured the last of his strength into it. He melted and mangled the golem's other arm. Then he went for the face. He angled his sorcerous beam at the red glow of the golem's right eye.

Boom!

A loud explosion rang out. A small portion of the golem's head had exploded. Sparks and shards of metal flew back along the sorcerous beam. The largest struck Talbon in the face. It bowled him over. He slammed to the floor and did not move.

The Lomerians surged forward and attacked the golem anew, weapons wild, as Ob dragged Talbon from the fray. The shard left an ugly wound. One of Talbon's eyes was mangled, maybe gone. His flesh was sliced from forehead to chin, shirt drenched in blood. His hands shook uncontrollably, though otherwise, he seemed unconscious.

The golem was nearly helpless; its limbs unresponsive. The men pounded it mercilessly. They struck it about the head, again and again, determined to destroy it. The clanking of metal on metal was deafening, akin to a dozen smiths gone mad. They didn't let up. Not for a moment.

Not until the golem's head cracked asunder. And the red glow from its remaining eye faded out — its mystic spark of life, forever extinguished.

The golem's head separated into two pieces — the face in the smaller piece, the back two thirds of the head in the other.

When the battle was over, and all was calm, McDuff picked up the face. He took it as a trophy. That didn't surprise the others at all, except that even that little bit of the thing weighed as much as a small man. Yet that did not deter the dwarf.

27

THE HOLLOW, FALSTAD MANOR

Year 801, 4th Age

Awareness returned. Azrael knew he was in trouble. He kept his eyes closed and fought the urge to move. He hoped he had made no sound or motion when he regained consciousness, but he just didn't know.

He hung upside down.

A rope was tied about his ankles. His head pounded with pain and felt numb — both at the same time. His legs burned and throbbed from the pressure.

What a fool he'd become. Distracted during a combat situation. Taken unawares and knocked out like a hapless victim of some common street mugging.

Azrael the Wise.

The Eternal.

Skilled of sword and magery beyond any mortal was he, yet defeated by a sick woman, mad out of her mind.

Trussed up like a rabbit after a hunt.

What a disgrace. What a joke. He'd become a joke.

Thank the gods the other arkons couldn't see him. What a wretch he'd become. He was glad for the pain. He deserved it. He wished it was worse.

He heard them eating.

Teeth tearing flesh; munching, chewing, slobbering like wild beasts.

He didn't know where he was.

He dared not open his eyes.

Not yet.

They'd either dragged him off, one or more of his fellows with him, and were feasting on them, or worse, they'd killed his whole party — all the hunters. Could they have done that? Had they grown that strong? That skilled?

He felt nauseous. He had a terrible thirst. He was so angry — at himself and at the infected. That's how he thought about them.

As infected.

Not as Pennebray.

Not as Lady Dahlia.

He had to think of them as things. Not as people. He decided that they weren't people any longer. It was the only way to bear it.

The guilt.

All his fault.

What to do?

Open his eyes for but a moment and take in the scene? If they noticed, they might finish him off immediately or else injure him further. Helpless to defend himself, hanging as he was. But perhaps they thought him dead. Should he say something? Engage them in conversation? Try to talk them back to reality, remind them of who they really are; appeal to whatever remnants of their humanity yet remained?

He could be very persuasive. And he could augment his formidable oratory skills with a bit of magery. But would it work? Was it worth the risk?

He knew better than to try it.

The bloodlust — the desire to eat flesh that he'd witnessed those last weeks, was too much for the infected to overcome. They were beyond all hope and reason. Without some dramatic medical cure they were lost forever.

His hands were free, dangling down. That was his chance. He had to act. Every moment he delayed he grew weaker.

But no, wait, perhaps there was yet another course. They were eating, ravenously, the infected were. Every moment he delayed, they grew more engorged. That would slow them, give him an advantage. Injured, restrained, he might need that. He would need that.

He hung there, biding his time. Listening.

Listening as they ate his men.

He only did that because it was clear that they were dead. He heard no whimpering, no pleadings, no one squirming to break free of their bonds. If they were alive, if there was a chance to save them, he would act, no matter the consequences. Or at least he'd want to act. Even if he couldn't.

His work was too important. Despite this terrible setback, the cure, the cure to the plague — the real plague, not just this bloodlust, was out there, somewhere. Only he was equipped to find

154

it. And it needed finding. He had to stay alive long enough to find that cure.

To perfect it.

To distribute it to the world.

He owed Midgaard that.

He was so close.

So close.

Closer than ever before.

After that was accomplished, that great deed, he wouldn't matter anymore. Then he could die, if such was his fate. Until then, he had to stay alive.

He waited a short time more, then chanced a glance. He opened his eyes for but a moment.

He hung in the grand foyer of Falstad Manor, almost at the very spot that the infected had fallen upon him. He dangled there, slowly spinning.

Two other men hung beside him.

He didn't have time to see who they were, and dared not turn his head for a better view, but by one's bulk, he had to be one of the blacksmiths. One infected (Pennebray) sat cross-legged on the floor, completely covered in blood, gore, entrails. Her belly bulged out before her, ten times its normal size. She chewed on a man's severed leg held between her small hands. Her attention on her meal, she didn't notice Azrael open his eyes. From the sounds, several other infected were behind him, though his slow spin would turn him toward their direction in a few moments.

Azrael had the strength to spring up and grasp the rope that held his feet. He knew he had that much energy left in him. That much at least.

Grasping that rope with one hand or both, taking the pressure off his legs, he might be able to pull his feet free. If he was fast enough, he might accomplish that unscathed.

But then what?

His legs were numb. He might not be able to stand, little less maneuver to fight. They might very well defeat him. Kill him.

And then what of the cure? What of Midgaard? And what if he couldn't get free fast enough? Then he'd have no chance at all.

There was only one course of action left open to him.

He had to wait.

He'd wait until they were fully engorged. They'd fall asleep; perhaps for days. He'd seen that many times before amongst their kind. They'd be near helpless.

It could work, if he waited. If he was patient. If he was lucky.

It would work.

Assuming they didn't have room enough to eat him before they had their fill. That was a risk. A terrible risk. But he had to take it. It was his best chance. Maybe his only chance.

And so he waited.

The price of carelessness and stupidity was high. He should never have been in that position. A rookie mistake to get caught unawares. If he hadn't walked into that ambush, his men wouldn't now be dead. His negligence had cost them their lives. But how many of them? Some or all?

What of old Refisal?

Had the little guy escaped?

Or did the gnome fill their bellies even now? His beard tickling their innards?

He put those thoughts aside. And he waited. He hung there for a goodly time. Thinking through tactical scenarios, planning his escape. Planning for every possible contingency.

Planning his vengeance.

28

THE DEAD FENS, THE KEEP

Year 1242, 4th Age
12th Year of King Tenzivel's Rule

Gabriel was about to face the golem alone again. Only a madman would do that. Or a brave hero. Or else a fool. He knew full well that his survival the first time was due as much to luck as it was to skill. And yet he tempted fate again.

He had to. From its actions inside the hall, there was no doubt in Gabriel's mind that the golem was determined to kill him. Him. That some magic set in motion when he failed to guess the password or pull the right lever compelled it to do so. He couldn't leave it be, for what he had told Aradon was true — the thing would follow him home. All the way to the northern mountains. All the way to Dor Eotrus. He couldn't allow that.

Better to face the creature now and be done with it, one way or another, than live in dread of it showing up who knows when.

Far worse than that dread, the golem would kill innocent people that it encountered along the way — anyone that tried to stop it, or that just crossed its path. Women. Children. Old Folk. It didn't matter to the golem. It had no feelings. No conscience. No regrets. And no fear.

If it ever reached Dor Eotrus, it would wreak bloody havoc. Who knows how many guardsmen and townsfolk would die before they put it down or contained it? Gabriel couldn't allow that — the death of innocents. Not on his account. Not on his conscience. He made it his mission to protect goodly folk wherever he could. The notion of getting them killed, however indirectly, was abhorrent to him. So abhorrent, that he risked all to face the golem then and there.

Alone.

As well he should. For this was a matter between he and Azrael or whoever else was behind this madness. It wasn't for ordinary folk. It was his responsibility, and his alone, to bring it to closure. To end it, and all the evils that Azrael apparently unleashed on the world.

It was bad enough that he had to leave the one-legged golem to his friends. The thing was damaged. Weak. Maybe dying. Growing weaker by the moment — the spark of sorcery that powered it, leaking out its stump and dispersing back unto the ether. As that sorcery spilled out, the golem's power ebbed, the same as that of a man suffering from blood loss. That gave the Lomerians the edge they needed. They'd find a way to end it. If not by brute force, then by Par Talbon's magic. They would take it down. Of this, Gabriel had little doubt.

The golem that he faced would prove much tougher. Nonetheless, he would find a way to destroy it.

There had to be a way.

There is always a way, Thetan used to say.

Gabriel would find it.

With the golem still trapped in the hole in the roof, Gabriel stepped through the ragged breach in the wall separating the great hall from the rooftop terrace, the big hammer back in his hands, the terrace deck spongy beneath his foot.

Nearly through the breach, Gabriel's eyes went wide as something flew toward him from across the roof. He twisted and dived to the terrace deck just as a large stone paver crashed into the wall above him — the impact so strong that the stone shattered into a hundred pieces and rained down, speckling his black hair with gray dust and stone fragments.

He looked up and rolled to the side, over and again, barely getting clear as another twenty pound hunk of stone crashed into the spot he'd just occupied. He was a ways away from the breach now, and out in the open, no cover to be found.

The golem already had another stone in hand. Its red eyes focused on him. All its will bent on destroying him.

29

THE HOLLOW, FALSTAD MANOR

Year 801, 4th Age

At some point, hanging there from his feet, Azrael either fell asleep or passed out. When awareness returned, all was silent. He still hung from the ropes. His head pounded all the harder. The numbness spread to his arms.

He opened his eyes.

It was dark.

Nighttime outside, for little light shown through the windows. Only a sliver of illumination provided by the moons. The sorry remnants of several candles burned about the room, abandoned here and there about the foyer's floor.

Only one man hung beside him.

Rintle Blacksmith. His throat slashed wide open.

The other man was gone.

Rintle was a tough man. He and his brother were the first to join up with Azrael and his guardsmen to go hunting for the infected. And now he was dead. Dead along with all the rest. Dead because of Azrael's mistakes. Because of his repeated blunders.

No one else was about. Azrael listened for a time, but no sounds came to his ears. Luck had been with him. Waiting had been the right decision, for the infected had eaten their fill and were gone. Just as he hoped.

He had no doubt that they'd be back. Maybe within moments. Maybe hours. Maybe days. Now was the time for escape.

With all his strength, Azrael flexed his abdomen, reached forward, and grasped the ropes that held him.

He pulled up, but his arms were partly numb. He didn't have the strength. He held himself there, his legs and back afire as the seconds ticked by and the circulation returned to his arms.

He pulled up on the rope with all the strength he could muster and tried to wrench his feet free. But the ropes were far too tight, his ankles abraded and bleeding, maybe swollen. He had to shift his weight and hold himself up by but one hand as he used the other to work the rope free of his ankles. All the while, he was as quiet as he could be, forcing himself not to grunt or breathe too loudly from the strain. He feared that the infected were still nearby, that they'd hear him. If they came at him while he was still restrained, he was finished.

He got one leg free. Dangling there, all his weight held by one arm, he got the second leg free. But he didn't drop. He held onto the rope with one hand for as long as he could, flexing and moving his toes, feet, and ankles all the while, trying to relieve the numbness and get the blood flowing. He feared if he dropped with his legs stiff and unresponsive, he'd break a foot or ankle or worse. He had no time for that.

When he couldn't hold the rope any longer, he switched to his other hand, and later, to both hands.

His muscles spent, his legs still partly numb, finally, he dropped to the floor, landed as lightly as he could, and rolled.

Luck was still with him. No bones broke. No tendons snapped. He rolled again, put his back to a wall and sat there, rubbing his legs, getting the blood circulating again. He didn't care if the infecteds came back while he was there.

He welcomed it.

It would save him the trouble of hunting them down. And he would hunt them down. Every one. And make them pay.

But they didn't come. He was alone.

He grabbed the nearest candlestick and in the moments that he sat there, his eyes were drawn to the floor, sticky and wet beneath him and all about the grand foyer of House Falstad. Even in the dim light, anyone looking at that floor could tell that people had died in battle there. More than a few. But no bodies were there now. All dragged away.

Except that they weren't dragged away. That was the true horror of it. They were eaten. Consumed in their totality at that very spot.

The tile floor was covered with fresh stains, excrement, and bones. Nothing remained that resembled a body. Or even parts of a body.

Except for the bones — they were the only large pieces left behind. Even they were broken open, the marrow sucked out.

Even the bones.

The horror of that was hard to fathom.

But perhaps even worse were the curious stain patterns strewn about the floor. The smears of dried or drying blood were everywhere — but not in any quantity. No blood was pooled here or there. No droplets even; not one.

The blood had been lapped up.

Every drop.

Those lapping tongues had left their trails in the stains that remained on the floor, the entirety of it licked almost clean.

Such an inhuman, monstrous hunger, insatiable, wanton, depraved. Azrael could not let such crimes — such madness — stand. He would not let them go unavenged.

To Helheim with curing the infected.

He'd kill them all.

30

THE DEAD FENS,
THE KEEP

Year 1242, 4th Age
12th Year of King Tenzivel's Rule

Still stuck in the hole in the roof, but full of fight was the golem, and smarter than Gabriel anticipated. Smart enough to pick up a rock and fling it with accuracy. It surely didn't have the intelligence of a man, but it was more than a simple automaton. More than a mindless thing. He should have expected that. Azrael was always the crafty one; he'd suffer no simpletons about him, not even if they were but golems.

The golem picked up another paver from the pile that lay around it, and flung it at Gabriel. And then another. This time, Gabriel saw them coming. And that made all the difference.

The accuracy of the golem's throws was uncanny. The power behind them and the speed at which the stones flew were beyond what any man could match.

But Gabriel was fast.

The brief moments the stones were aloft were time enough for him to react. He twisted, ducked, or dodged as need be. One stone crashed just next to him, and then another. What bits and shards hit him, of no consequence.

Gabriel stepped forward even as the golem threw another stone, and then another, and another. He dodged them all despite the closing distance between them.

And then Gabriel's hammer descended on the golem. The golem twisted and ducked with surprising speed, and suffered only a glancing blow to the side of its head. The golem's arms lashed out, but Gabriel had already backpedaled out of reach. He recognized he could not stand toe to toe with the golem — a creature whose arms alone weighed several times his entire body weight.

The golem stretched towards him, wrenching its back to its limit, its fingers flexing, trying with all its might to reach Gabriel. To grab him. To wring the life out of him. But it found only empty air.

Gabriel circled around, faster than the golem could turn, but careful to keep his footing sure on the damaged roof. Then he came in again. This time, the hammer landed squarely atop the golem's head, all Gabriel's power behind it. So strong was that strike that it flattened the top of the creature's head.

Two things happened at once: the golem fell through the hole, and the hole grew larger. The portion of roof beneath Gabriel's feet gave way, but he skipped back to solid surface. Even as he did, that portion of the roof gave way too, and Gabriel fell. He twisted in the air and stretched to hold on to the edge, but found no stable purchase. All he received for his efforts were stone pavers hitting his face as they slid toward and fell into the breach.

Gabriel ignored those bruises, bent his knees, and braced for the inevitable impact. He looked down but couldn't see anything but blackness below.

Then he hit.

31

THE HOLLOW, FALSTAD MANOR

Year 801, 4th Age

Azrael put his ear to the door of the antechamber that adjoined Falstad Manor's grand foyer.

Nothing.

No sound crept from within. No light escaped through the door. He had no idea what he might find within.

Nothing, perhaps.

An ambush?

Or a group of engorged infecteds, sleeping off their terrible meal.

In the end, it didn't matter. He was going in. He had no weapon, save for fist and foot. They would serve if need be. He held a candlestick on-high, opened the door, and stepped in as silently as he could.

He almost tripped on the first body. Startled, he jumped back.

It was an infected. Dead. Lying on its back. Multiple wounds about his head and chest from blade and bludgeon.

The hunters work, it had to be.

But what else lurked in the dark corners of that chamber? The room was pitch black, illuminated only by the frail light of the two lonely candles, halfway melted, that sat in his candlestick.

He heard no breathing. Felt no presence. And his ankh was quiet.

He raised the candlestick higher and took another step in.

A second body lay shoulder to shoulder with the last. Another dead infected, its head staved in.

And another past that one.

None were gnawed upon. That confirmed Azrael's suspicions that the infected didn't eat their own. Why? He had no idea. They had no qualms about eating their own family members, their own children, but they'd not take a single nibble of another infected. An odd thing.

The antechamber's floor told the tale of the battle — including why his hunters lost. In total, nine infected lay there, the bodies carefully arrayed on their backs, side by side. All dead. All with terrible wounds. Limbs missing. Heads cut off or staved in. Sternums punctured. The hunters had made a good account of themselves indeed, to have felled so many monsters before they went down.

The condition of the infecteds' bodies implied that they had some respect for the dead. Their dead. That they felt some affinity for each other. Why? And did that mean something? Could Azrael use that to his advantage? How the infecteds held onto such emotions while dispensing with every other semblance of humanity, Azrael could not say. He could not grasp it.

He felt a strange mix of emotions at the sight of those corpses. The death itself, the wounds, didn't move him. He'd seen so much of that for so long, it stirred nothing in him, especially considering that all of the dead were infected — — and by Azrael's thinking, no longer human. No longer worthy of compassion or pity.

But Azrael felt pride that his men had taken them on and had brought so many down. So too did he feel a terrible guilt, for he was knocked out in the first moments of the melee, leaving his men without their leader. Without their best fighter. Their champion.

How they must have felt. And yet still they fought like tigers.

How many died protecting his unconscious body from the fangs of the infecteds?

Azrael knew not. In truth, he didn't want to know.

And why hadn't he foreseen that there were so many infected left? He'd thought that only Lady Dahlia and Pennebray remained at large. He'd blundered again.

Again.

First with his bungled cure that was no cure, but a plague in itself. Then he failed to connect the "cured" with the killings. How obvious that connection now seemed. Only a blind fool could have missed it. He supposed that's what he was; what he'd become.

And now he'd gotten all his men killed. Led them straight into an ambush. An amateur's mistake.

What a fool he'd become, the great man. The last living arkon of Azathoth, or so he presumed. Now he was naught but a fool. A victim. A wretched, pathetic thing to be outwitted and defeated by the sick and depraved, the no longer human. It was disgusting. Embarrassing. Humiliating.

And it couldn't be undone.

A pile of gear lay in one corner of the antechamber. Armor, weapons, clothing, packs. All the gear and equipment that the hunters had on their persons when they were ambushed.

Azrael's sword, helm, and trident were amongst that sorry, bloodsoaked heap. He reclaimed them. They were all he needed to take his revenge.

He could never make amends. Never undo what he'd done. But at least he could have revenge, however bittersweet that always was.

Triber Blacksmith's axe was in the heap. So was Bron Mason's hammer, and Rit Bowman's bow and arrows. All of the hunters' gear was there.

Except for Refisal's. Good old Refisal. Azrael searched the heap for any sign, sigil, or scrap of cloth of the old gnome's, but there was none to be found. The old grouch had slipped their grasp! He must have made the door and taken off back to Virent Hall. Hopefully unharmed. Azrael was thankful for that. More than he could say. The old gnome had been his assistant and confidant for more years than he could remember. It seemed like he was always there, back unto the beginning. The only true friend that he had left.

It warmed Azrael's heart that the old man was still alive.

Fully equipped again, Azrael decided he wouldn't leave Falstad Manor until he'd killed every infected that remained there. No exceptions for Dahlia or even Pennebray. After what they'd done, they deserved no mercy, no quarter.

32

THE DEAD FENS,
THE KEEP

Year 1242, 4th Age
12th Year of King Tenzivel's Rule

The fall through the hole in the roof was a drop of five or six meters. Gabriel fell straight down and landed on his feet, happily on an even surface despite the debris all about. The landing was jarring and painful, but he escaped injury. That was lucky. Very lucky considering he didn't see the ground before he hit it.

Hand and forearm protecting his head, he scrambled to get out from under the hole — for more stone pavers rained down and crashed to the floor as the terrace's roof buckled.

As quick as Gabriel was, he wasn't quick enough, and his luck ran out. One stone hit him squarely on the shoulder, nearly bringing him to his knees. Another grazed his back. But it was the third that did the most damage.

It hit him atop his head. His protective arm absorbed much of the blow, but not enough.

A searing, burning pain assailed his head. He stumbled forward, somehow keeping hold of the hammer. He was dizzy and he could barely see anything: the space was dark; his eyes teared, and a veil of dust caused by the collapse enshrouded everything.

And then the blood streamed down his forehead. Fast. A deep or wide wound. He tasted it on his lips.

He hated head wounds. He ignored it — the pain, the blood, just as he'd trained himself to do. Just as he'd done many times before. He'd deal with it later. It wouldn't kill him, it wasn't bad enough, but the golem might, so he put the pain aside. Even for Gabriel that wasn't an easy thing to do, but unlike most men, if he put his mind to it, he could do it. He had the discipline.

He was thankful that he still had use of his arm. The stone had bruised his shoulder, and it throbbed, but it wasn't broken. One armed against that thing, he'd have no chance. No chance at all.

He couldn't see the golem. Or much of anything besides the wide shaft of light that streamed down from the hole in the ceiling. It revealed fallen wood beams and boards, rotted and fractured, the stone pavers from above, and a jumbled pile of red bricks — the fallen remnants of an arched ceiling long neglected.

Everything else, all around him, nothing but black. Nothing but the dark. There were no windows in the place. No way to tell even how big the room was. The air was damp, still, and stagnant, and stank of mold and mildew. The floor was wet. The place surely hadn't been used in long years — at least not by anything alive.

But where was the golem? Did it lurk just behind him, silently waiting to strike? Or was it on the other side of the room, damaged from the fall? Buried under the debris? Did it even know he had fallen too? Mayhap the thing was broken, dead, a lifeless hunk of metal, as it should be.

He doubted it. But he didn't know.

Most men took time to adjust to the dark, their eyes slowly dilating to let in more light. Gabriel's eyes adjusted almost immediately. But that didn't help. With all the dust in the air and the streaming blood from his cut, he couldn't see much. Unless the golem stepped into that lightwell, he'd not see it at all.

He'd have to rely on his hearing. And thanks to his head wound, his ears weren't working correctly just then — they were all plugged up and both ears rang with high-pitched tones. He made out the shouts and cries of battle in the distance — no doubt, his friends still battled old One Leg. But that was all he heard, and barely that.

It was even hard to breathe in that place, with all the dust in the air. He fought to keep from coughing. He had to remain silent or else give away his position.

Or did he?

Did the golem even have the power of hearing? Did it go by sight alone? Or did it employ some strange, esoteric sense unknown to man?

A moment later, he felt . . . something. A hint of vibration from the floor; the slightest movement of the air. He knew he should have heard something along with that, but he didn't. Thank the head wound for that.

Something was behind him. Just off to the right. How close, he didn't know. The golem or something else?

He felt the vibration again. A moment later, the slightest breeze. It was a step that caused it. Something heavy had taken a step. One and then another. Slowly. Ever so slowly did it move. So carefully. Trying to remain silent. Trying to stay hidden. It had to be the golem.

It was stalking him. Since when did golems stalk men? Not known for subtlety or stealth were golems. They'd just come straight at you. He'd never heard of one acting like this. But where Azrael was concerned, little surprised him.

It was close, and smarter than he expected, and perhaps even more dangerous. But did it see him? Did it know where he was?

Another step did he sense, the air moving faster that time.

Gabriel ducked. He didn't see a blow coming; didn't hear one either. Somehow, he just knew an attack was incoming. Call it a warrior's intuition.

The golem's arm swept through the air just over his head.

Gabriel spun and leaped into the light, vaulting over debris. That's when he realized how badly he was hurt. His head felt twice its normal size and he was dizzy. He didn't remember when he'd lost his helm. Probably when the thing tossed him into the wall. Nobody was ever able to hit him in the head when his helm was on, but the minute it's off, his skull gets battered from all sides. Figures. His limbs didn't want to respond;

his reactions, dulled. The room swayed; he barely kept his feet.

He backpedaled; tried to put as much of the lit area between him and the golem as he could. At least he'd see it coming. Gabriel readied his hammer and waited for the charge. It would come straight at him now. No respite until it or Gabriel were dead.

Except that it didn't charge.

It didn't follow him at all. Instead, the room went quiet again.

Gabriel turned his head this way and that; ignoring the dizziness that that brought on, he tried to pick up any hint of movement, any sound. There was nothing. Nothing but his own breathing and the pulsing of blood at his temples. His heart raced. He didn't dare move his feet. He didn't dare give away his position. If only he could see it. If only he had a torch. Or something else that might help. Anything.

Gabriel felt the vibration again, but from which direction, he couldn't say. His head was spinning. He felt disoriented. Almost like he was floating. Damn head injury.

That little flutter of the flooring came again and again, a few seconds between. Still he wasn't certain from where. It crept along, out there in the black. Biding its time. He'd never heard of a stealthy golem before. Damn that Azrael.

Movement on his left.

Gabriel ducked again.

A paving stone flew past his face.

And then more. One after another. They flew out of the darkness. A half dozen of them. More.

Gabriel dodged. Ducked. Spun. No cover to hide behind. No shield. He felt like his feet were glued to the ground, his movements slow, clumsy, and sloppy. Yet they were deft enough. No pavers hit him cleanly, despite the golem's skill.

A stone ricocheted off the hammer's haft and slammed into Gabriel's chest, knocking him back several steps. If not for his breastplate it would have staved in his ribs. While Gabriel reeled from the blow, the golem barreled out of the darkness. It saw its chance and it didn't hesitate. It charged straight for him, picking up speed with each step; it crushed or bowled over everything in its path.

Gabriel leaped aside at the last moment.

The golem ground to a halt in but three steps.

Gabriel's hammer struck it, behind its right knee. Unbalanced, the golem stumbled back. Gabriel shoved the hammer's haft between the golem's legs, tripping it. It fell backward as a cut tree.

Gabriel avoided the golem's flailing arm, stepped close, and raised the hammer high. He brought it down with all his strength on the golem's right knee. With a fierce clang of metal, the joint dented, but did not crack or shatter.

Out of the corner of his eye, Gabriel saw the golem's right arm flailing a moment before it hit him. He twisted and avoided the brunt of the blow, but still that weighty arm hit him unbelievably hard. Gabriel felt himself flying through the air.

33

THE HOLLOW, FALSTAD MANOR

Year 801, 4th Age

Azrael made his way into the main ballroom. Still was it filled with corpses, the stench unbearable. Many lay as they fell, weeks ago, their throats torn out, their hearts ripped from their chests. But that place was not just a morgue or a murder site. It was a larder. A pantry for monsters of ravenous, unholy appetites.

Some of the bodies had been gnawed upon. An arm missing here, a leg there. More than a few with great chunks of flesh eaten away. Most were little more than gruesome heaps of broken bones, matted hair, and shredded clothing. That was a hard thing to see. Even for a man that had walked untold battlefields. Even after all that Azrael had witnessed during the previous weeks. Bile rose in his throat. He wanted to vomit. To run from there, far from there, and never look back.

But he didn't. He wouldn't. It was his task to stop the bloodlust, one way or another. He had to. There was no one else. He created the disease, however unwittingly, and he would end it.

Leaving the ballroom behind, Azrael skulked through the halls, silent as a mouse — even the old wooden floorboards dared not creak under his light step. What use that silence was, he wasn't certain, for his way was lit by the candlestick he carried. For all its worth, that tiny flame gave away his position, making it as much a liability as it was a necessity.

Azrael's search brought him up the grand stair that led off from the foyer. It was at the top of those steps that he heard it.

Laughter.

It was distant — from far back in the bowels of the sprawling manor house. Its origin, he traced to the upstairs parlor — a large room, high ceilinged and richly accoutered. It overlooked the rear garden.

The parlor's door was slightly ajar. Azrael moved toward it like a ghost, armor notwithstanding. He stood in the hall nearby the door for some moments, listening.

The infected were in there. Many of them. Laughing and carrying on. They'd just murdered and eaten his men, and yet they were laughing.

Laughing.

Azrael's blood began to boil. He felt a rage well up inside him. But he took a deep breath and suppressed it. He pushed the anger back down. He needed to keep his head clear. To maintain his composure.

He put his feelings aside and listened. The infecteds' language was base and foul, their jokes raunchy and obscene. Gutter speech.

Nothing they said was of any use. No mention of any more of their kind hidden about. No discussion of grand plans or unsavory secrets.

Azrael suspected that they didn't have any. That they were as animals. Cunning. Deadly. But living from moment to moment. Like wild beasts.

And when a beast became a man eater, there was only one course of action. To put it down.

The parlor was candlelit. From what little Azrael could see, the infected lounged about on furniture and floor in various states of undress. Liquor bottles were strewn everywhere. They were drunk. And at least some were engorged. Azrael smelled the alcohol, thick in the air. He smelled the blood. He smelled the scent of death. A grand party for the wicked and depraved. Nothing left of their humanity to restrain their base longings and unholy cravings.

Azrael pushed the door open with his trident's tip. A long, whiny squeak did the door hinges make.

Black eyes and bared fangs greeted him as some of the infected went silent and looked over. Others were oblivious, awash in their debauchery. In all, at least two dozen of them haunted that room. Two dozen brazen killers of superhuman speed and strength. Things with no conscience. No inhibitions. No regrets.

Pennebray was there. Fully engorged. Slumped against a wall, unconscious, an empty liquor bottle in hand, her belly impossibly large before her, stretching out past her knees. Fifty, perhaps even a hundred pounds of flesh must she have consumed. Several other infected sat or lay to either side of her, similarly bloated and slumbering.

181

Lady Dahlia was across the room, naked and intimately intertwined with two other infected: one male, one female — each of their bellies were bloated and stuck out a foot before them, the women's breasts bloated to more than twice their normal size. Several other males lined up behind Dahlia awaiting their turns.

Dahlia looked up at Azrael as he stood there, in those few moments while the room froze. She didn't seem surprised to see him. If anything, she looked happy. "Join us, wizard," she said as she turned her body, offering herself to him. "Be one with us. Be one with me. You're the one I really want. We should rule together."

At once disgusted and enthralled, Azrael felt the unmistakable tug of her magic affecting his mind, influencing him to obey her, to please her, to be one with her. For reasons unknown, her power, her influence, was far stronger, far harder to resist than that of the two women in the dungeon. But this time, the ankh was under his armor and rested against the bare skin of his chest. It did not fail him. With its help, his mind, his will, remained his own; the struggle, intense, but brief — lasting but moments.

How the disease, the bloodlust, had a magic to it, how it could reach out from an infected to a healthy man's mind and sap his will, made no sense to Azrael. Never had he encountered any illness like it. He wanted to study it. To probe its secrets and plumb its depths. To bend it to his will.

But he knew he couldn't. He would not blunder again. Not again.

Azrael stepped into the room and closed the door behind him. His eyes were cold as northern ice. His resolve, unforgiving as the sea.

He reached back and set the door's deadbolt.

No one was leaving.

34

CITY OF GEMORRDA

THE AGE OF MYTH AND LEGEND

When Gabriel opened his eyes, he sat amongst boulders, high on a hill overlooking a vast city of large stone buildings, tall and stately, but in the grip of chaos. Of death.

A storm of screaming fireballs rained down on that metropolis from on-high. They pounded buildings from one side of the city to the other. Great or small, when those fireballs hit, the buildings exploded and collapsed, crushing and burning everything about them.

Other structures were ablaze, their roofs or walls staved in, masonry tumbling down. Great swaths of the city were fully engulfed in flames. People trapped on roofs screamed for help that would never come. Countless others jumped from roofs and windows, choosing a quick death rather than endure the horror of the heat and the flames.

On the ground, people fled screaming in all directions. Men. Women. Children. Unarmed. Frightened out of their wits. Dust and ash covered their faces, filled their lungs, obscured their vision. Most had nothing but the clothes on their backs. Some shouted for their loved ones, desperately looking this way and that as they ran. Others pulled their beloveds along, babies in arms, old folk hobbling behind. Many ran alone; most of them didn't look back.

The great lord Azathoth, the one true god, sat silently on a boulder, glowing all in white as was his wont, his expression stern. The lord's Arkon, Thetan, was at Azathoth's right hand, Mithron at his left, as was their place. Azrael was there. So was Bhaal. So too was Uriel, Mikel, Arioch, and more.

"The city is at heel, Lord," said Azrael the Wise, his magnificent green trident in hand, as he gazed down at the destruction, his emerald plate armor polished to a sheen, as was that of all his companions.

Gabriel turned to observe the lord's reaction, and saw that Thetan did the same, but Azathoth offered no reaction, no reply.

"There is much of value in the city," said Azrael. "Items the faithful can use to spread your good word."

It took courage to question the lord. It took conviction. Such things were not done lightly, and not without risk, even for an Arkon.

That moment was when Gabriel first knew that Azrael was of like mind with he and Thetan.

Thetan knew it too.

"No longer," said Azathoth. "It will all be destroyed. Consumed by flame. A just penance for their defiance. And for their sins."

"My lord," said Thetan, "are there not many innocent folk amongst that multitude? Folk worthy of your mercy?"

"A fair question," said Azathoth. "And I thank you for asking it, most loyal and honorable Thetan."

"How could there not be good people amongst so many, you might ask?" said Azathoth. The lord looked around to make certain that he had the attention of all the Arkons, which of course, he did. When he spoke, everyone listened, though not all heard or heeded.

"I will tell you," said Azathoth. "They are corrupt, base, degenerate folk. Wanton sinners that care nothing for others and only for themselves. Thieves, covetors, liars, and sadists. Of all the tribes of men on Midgaard, those of Gemorrda are amongst the lowest, the foulest."

"And yet, despite all their flaws, I blessed them with my good word, so that they could redeem themselves and join us on the righteous path. Join my faithful. My kingdom.

"I extended the olive branch of peace. I offered them forgiveness for their countless transgressions. I offered them absolution.

"Moreover, I offered them my protection.

"Most importantly, I offered them my love.

"My love!" shouted Azathoth, his face and white robes shading to red for some moments.

"You saw how they defied me," said Azathoth. "You heard their insults. You saw them worshiping their craven idols — the false gods of their puny imaginations. They had their chance — more chances than they deserve."

"And still they defy me," said Azathoth. "Even now do they curse me. Listen. Listen to their blasphemies."

Azathoth went silent for some moments as they all listened. Through the cries, and screams, the crackling flames, and the myriad explosions, Gabriel could not make out any individual's words, foul or fair. He supposed that Azathoth could, for he was the lord and had powers unknown.

Azathoth's voice was quieter when he spoke again, though just as stern as before. "For them, there can only be the void. Only the void."

"What of the children?" said Azrael.

Azathoth paused and turned his gaze on Azrael. "Do you beseech me to spare them, trusted Arkon?"

"The innocent should not be made to suffer for the sins of the corrupt," said Azrael, his words slow; he struggled to get them out, but said them with conviction.

"Well do you remember my words," said Azathoth. "I am pleased by that. Let me assure you, all of you," he said, addressing his gathered Arkons, "that those few innocents amongst them will be spared. I have already taken steps to do that. But of the innocent, you must understand, there are very few, even amongst the smallest children, for they have been schooled from infancy to hate me. To hate all that I stand for. To hate the way of life of my people, my children. All to curry favor with the dark powers of the lower realms and the fantasies of their warped idolatry."

Azathoth held out his right arm and pointed at the city. "There lies a city more corrupt, more evil, than any Midgaard has ever known. In destroying it, we're doing the right thing. The just thing. Do you understand?" he said to Azrael.

"Yes, my lord," said Azrael.

"Mikel," said Azathoth. "Send forth your cavalry and bring down those who've fled. Put them to the sword. Trample them underfoot. One and all. And fear not in the slaying. For those few good folk amongst them are already well protected. Even if your lances and blades found them, they will do them no harm."

Azathoth moved to another vantage point where he could better watch the slaughter as Mikel's cavalry thundered into action, thousands strong. Gabriel observed as Azrael watched the lord, seeing him, truly seeing him, as if for the first time. Azrael's face grew grim and grimmer still.

The cavalry, heavy horse, thundered down on the fleeing civilians. Their charge shook the entire hill. The knights lowered their lances as they neared the stragglers — old folks and women with children. Gabriel turned away. He couldn't watch. Not again. Never again. He hoped that the lord didn't notice. But it wouldn't change anything. He'd not watch such slaughter ever again. If only he had the power to stop it. To end the madness. But he didn't. Not now. Not yet. But soon.

Such a strange sound those horses made as they galloped — a loud, metallic pounding. As if they stepped slowly, unevenly, instead of galloping. It didn't make sense. It made Gabriel's head hurt.

Gabriel opened his eyes. The golem lumbered toward him, limping on its damaged leg, each step shaking the floor, its metallic thumping reverberating through the place.

35

THE HOLLOW, FALSTAD MANOR, THE UPSTAIRS PARLOR

Year 801, 4th Age

Azrael's sword sped from left to right. Blocked the thrust. Even so, his opponent's blade nicked his breastplate. The next slash came in all the faster. Azrael's sword, a blur; it parried the blow.

Three more strikes came in equally fast: high, low, then high again. For all his speed, twice that of men called experts, the third strike slammed into his breastplate. It raked across with a skirling rending of metal and flying sparks. That blow was so hard, and cut so deep, Azrael expected to feel the terrible burning of a flesh wound, and the wet of his own blood dripping down the inside of his armor.

But, somehow, the armor held, if barely.

"Give up now, and I'll slay you quickly," said the infected. "You have no chance against me."

That was Jaros Tull — the hulking captain of the mercenary company that Azrael hired to help him put down the spread of the bloodlust. Jaros and several others went missing two weeks prior. Now their fate was known.

A natural leader of men, Jaros was the most skilled warrior amongst Azrael's hunters, far better even than the guardsmen that Azrael had trained. Now, as an infected, Jaros was twofold faster and stronger than ever before. And he knew it.

And Azrael was tired. Wounded. Spent. His once green armor was red — awash of blood and gore. His helm was gone. His trident too. His face, slashed. Blood in his eyes, his mouth, his nose. His right arm was damaged, he didn't know how badly, and his head pounded.

But Azrael had done his damage. He'd taken his revenge.

The parlor was a scene of blood and carnage that in some ways surpassed the horror of the grand ballroom. Blood covered every surface: floor, walls, and ceiling alike. Bodies lay everywhere, many atop one another. Severed limbs and severed heads lay scattered about. The infected lay in heaps. Victims of Azrael's vengeance. His fury.

Only Jaros remained on his feet.

The mercenary waited in the shadows throughout the whole of the battle.

He watched as the infected surged toward Azrael soon after he entered. He watched as Azrael drove them back, fighting like a man possessed.

He watched as Azrael cut down one infected after another after another. Even for the wizard it was difficult. Blows that would've killed any normal person often had no effect on the infected.

But Azrael had the speed.

The strength. The experience.

A trident that could puncture and tear apart their hearts.

A sword that could sever limbs or head.

And the skills to use them to their fullest effects.

None could stand against him and live.

Jaros watched as several infected made for the door, and pounded on it trying to escape, too panicked or confused to work the lock, which would've opened for them if they had but sense to try. He watched Azrael cut them down from behind without mercy.

And still he watched as Azrael drove the trident through Dahlia's chest.

But then, when the wizard threw down his trident and pulled his sword, ready to take the woman's head, Jaros saw his chance.

Azrael hesitated.

The ice of his eyes melted for a but a moment as he looked at Dahlia. Compassion shown through. Weakness.

That's when Jaros attacked.

He threw his initial strikes and made his threats. They didn't faze Azrael.

After that, the duel began.

Slash and slice. Kick and dodge. Headbutts and fangs.

And then Azrael's sword sliced deep into Jaros's chest.

The infected staggered back. As Azrael came in to finish him, Jaros unleashed a spinning kick that sent Azrael's sword flying from his grasp.

Azrael spun and slammed his fist against the back of Jaros's neck — a blow that would've put most any man down. But it had no effect.

"She's mine," said Jaros. "You'll never have her. Never."

Jaros lunged in, and tried to bite the wizard, his mouth opening unnaturally wide, his teeth, long and sharp. Azrael held him back with one hand and punched with the other. An uppercut to the jaw.

No effect.

As Jaros pressed forward, Azrael grabbed the infected's hands, to keep the claws off him. They grappled, hands locked together. Jaros's claws bit into the back of Azrael's hands. They struggled. Strength against strength. Each determined to win. Each determined to kill. An even match were they.

Jaros's jaws snapped shut, over and over, and his neck stretched to its limit as he tried to bite the wizard. "I'll drink you dry," he said. Suddenly, Azrael fell backward, pulling Jaros down with him and kicking upward as he rolled. Jaros flew a dozen feet across the room and landed by the back window.

Azrael was up in an instant. He ran forward. Just as Jaros made his feet, Azrael vaulted forward and dropkicked him in the chest. Jaros flew backward, crashed into and through the window. Out into the night did he plummet. Only the stone terrace far below to break his fall.

The first slivers of the dawn shown over the horizon as Azrael leaned out the shattered window and looked down at Jaros, sprawled some twenty-five feet below, his limbs, his neck twisted and bent. Dead for certain. As Azrael looked down, the hairs on the back of his neck stood up. Death lurked behind him. He felt it. He sensed it. He knew it was there. He turned to face it.

THE DEAD FENS, THE KEEP

Year 1242, 4th Age
12th Year of King Tenzivel's Rule

Every bone in Gabriel's body hurt. He struggled to rise. Bricks lay piled about him, one perched on his shoulder. As he pulled himself to his feet, he realized that the golem's blow had flung him into the wall several yards from where he had stood. He hit so hard that the wall partially collapsed around him. No common man would have gotten up from that. They'd be dead.

He still had the battle hammer, but what good would it do him? His mind raced for some tactic to use against the golem. He had to disable it. To get it off its feet and keep it down. Then he'd have time to figure out how to destroy it.

As he made his feet, the golem swiped at him. It raked his cloak with its fingers but couldn't find purchase. Gabriel pulled away, his muscles barely responsive. He stumbled toward a column beneath the edge of the hole in the roof, blood streaming from his nose. The golem followed.

A third of the way there, Gabriel turned toward the golem. "You're too slow to get me," he shouted. "Worthless hunk of rusty metal. That's what you are."

The golem lunged, but Gabriel spun and slipped its grasp. He raced for the column, all his will and energies focused on speed. The golem charged after him, picking up speed with each stride.

Two steps from the column, Gabriel was in a full sprint. The golem was on him, merely a step behind — just where Gabriel wanted him.

At the last moment, Gabriel dodged aside and sped past the column. The golem was not so agile. It rammed the column shoulder first. The twelve inch square timber snapped in two. And the brick arch roof structure crashed down just as Gabriel hoped it would. It dropped directly atop the golem.

Although he chanced a glance back, Gabriel never slowed his stride. He ran blindly into the darkness as the roof collapsed around him. He had no idea what lay before him. He might slam head first into a wall, or fall into a pit, or barrel into who knows what. He had no idea. Too dark to see. And it didn't matter. He had to move from where he was or else be buried in rubble.

In a moment, the collapse overtook him. In a last, desperate attempt to avoid being crushed, he dived, covered his head, and hoped for the best.

The collapse halted when it reached the next line of columns, which Gabriel's dive had put him just past. As fate would have it, very little debris fell on him.

Gabriel pulled his shirt up over his mouth and breathed through it to filter out as much of the dust as he could. The roof hole now much larger;

far more light entered the hall. As the dust began to settle, he made his way back whence he'd come, walking atop the debris. He searched for the hammer. He had to find it. If the golem wasn't dead, that was the only weapon he had that might damage it. He could pound it all day with wood, or brick, or stone, and do it no harm at all.

Luck was with him. He saw the glint of metal as the sun shone through the roof hole. He climbed over the debris and plucked the hammer from a pile of brick where it lay half buried.

Bricks shifted and fell not far away.

The golem.

It stirred. It was alive. It was trying to get to its feet.

Gabriel raced recklessly to it — no time for sure footing or caution. He had to launch his next attack before the thing stood up.

He slammed the great hammer into the golem's jaw. Partially stuck in the debris, it made no defense. Then he hit it again. And again.

The golem tried to block the blows with one of its arms, the other disabled from the collapse. Gabriel battered its hand away, and then maneuvered around it, to where he had free reign to attack. The golem's legs were obstructed by the debris and it couldn't turn around fast enough.

Gabriel hit it atop the head. He ignored his own pain. His muscles and bones screaming for him the stop. Begging for him to run.

He hit the golem in the head again. Then again. And again. And again.

He didn't stop.

He just pounded away.

The golem reacted; it fought back, but less and less so as Gabriel kept up his pounding. Gabriel dodged all the golem's blows, but nearly all of his hit home. How the hammer didn't break, how the haft didn't snap, Gabriel had no idea.

How long he stood there and hit the golem, over and again, he never knew.

How many times he hit it, he could never say. He only knew that at one point, its head cracked in two. When that happened, the golem immediately went lifeless and fell face first to the floor.

But Gabriel wasn't done. He hit it as hard as he could about the head, neck, and back, at least ten more times. Maybe twenty. Maybe more. He didn't know. He didn't care. All that mattered was that the golem would never move again.

And it didn't.

When he looked up, the other Lomerians were there, standing around him. For how long, he knew not. Aradon. Ob. Artol. Malvegil and McDuff. They looked spent. And they looked afraid.

But their eyes weren't affixed on the dead golem. They stared at him. At Gabriel.

Was that fear in their eyes? Did they think that he snapped? That he'd fallen into a berserker rage? Were they afraid of him?

Well that they should be.

They'd come down a rope to help him.

But he needed no help.

Not then.

Not ever.

37

THE HOLLOW, FALSTAD MANOR, THE UPSTAIRS PARLOR

Year 801, 4th Age

The death that lurked behind Azrael was Dahlia. Lady Dahlia. Or at least, the creature that Dahlia had become. Still alive was she. She groaned in pain and hobbled toward Azrael, snarling, claws bared.

How she stood at all, Azrael couldn't fathom. The wounds he inflicted on her would have killed any normal person, but not her. Not an infected. In fact, her wounds seemed half healed already.

"I forgive you, my wizard," said Dahlia when their eyes met; her voice, hoarse and weak. Those first words came from her mouth, and Azrael heard them with his ears, just as with any sound, but most of the rest of what she said echoed only in his head, somehow transferred directly from her brain to his, no voice or ears needed.

"It's not too late for us," she said in his mind, her voice now sounding its normal self: melodic, sultry, enticing. "We can still be together, just as I promised. I forgive you for what you've done to me. It was a mistake. You knew not what you were doing. And never fear, my love, my wounds will soon heal. I will soon be whole again. And then you can have me. Take me. Whenever you desire. However you desire. As often as you desire. I'll be yours forever, wizard. We can rule this world, together."

Azrael's eyes were stone cold. He'd not be corrupted or fooled by a monster. By a thing.

He picked up his sword. It didn't matter how desirable she was. How much he lusted for her. He wouldn't listen. He wouldn't succumb to her temptations.

"I loved you from the start," she said. "From the moment I saw you. You must believe me. I would not lie to you. Not about this. Not about my feelings. Not about my heart."

Azrael felt the unnatural tug on his emotions, the influence she somehow exerted on his mind. He felt his will bend. He tried to fight it. But what was the point? He wanted her. Wanted her from the first, just as she wanted him. There was no denying that. Not anymore. Not to himself. Not to her. What would be the point?

He looked her body up and down. He needed her. To have her. He longed for her embrace. He longed to take her that very moment.

The blood that covered them both didn't matter. The gore. The excrement. The stench. They didn't matter. He'd wallow in it. He'd lap it off her. He'd drink every drop and savor it. He'd be like her. One with her. A beast. A monster. They'd devour the world together. They'd drink it dry. Forever. His grand destiny at last achieved. His greatness, at last returned to him.

And then he heard a voice

A woman's voice it was. But not Dahlia's. So familiar was that voice, yet he could not name her. He could not picture her face.

"Remember who you are," said the voice. "Remember."

Azrael was confused. He was on his knees. Dahlia before him. Inviting him closer. Begging him to continue. To touch her. To be with her.

So beautiful was she. More beautiful than any woman he'd ever seen. Or ever dreamed of, in waking life or fantasy. Her hair, so red, so luxurious. Her eyes, of limitless depths of love and wisdom. Her breasts, grown huge. Five times their natural size and growing larger by the moment. As large as he wanted. His hands were on them. Caressing them. His pants were unfastened.

He was hers. And she was his. Nothing could stop them now. Nothing.

"Remember," said the voice.

Then he felt a fleeting touch on his shoulder. A touch that sent a tingle of electricity from his head to his toes, from his manhood, to his soul. And a momentary glimpse of green skin and a green and yellow dress teased the corner of his eye. A girl. A woman. So fleeting was her image. But he knew her. He'd always known her. And she'd always known him. Back unto the beginning.

"You are Azrael the Wise," said the voice. "Remember who you are."

And then he did.

He punched Dahlia in the jaw, even as she lunged toward him, fangs bared and hungry. He hit her again and again. After five blows, she fell back, unconscious. He turned this way and that, but the green woman was nowhere to be seen. Who she was, he had no idea. Even that fleeting memory of her disappeared from his mind and did not return until their next meeting.

Azrael stood and picked up his sword. Dahlia lay helpless before him. It was time to end this. He raised the sword—

THE DEAD FENS,
THE KEEP

Year 1242, 4th Age
12th Year of King Tenzivel's Rule

Gabriel pulled himself hand over hand up the rope that the Lomerians dropped through the hole in the terrace's roof. They wanted to pull him up, but he'd have none of it. He climbed, the same as most of the others. At the top, rising up behind and above the main hall, he spied a slender stone turret. That's where the warlock had to be hiding. The last redoubt of the master of the dead.

Ob found the turret's hidden door off in a dark corner of the main hall; McDuff got it open — quietly that time. One last spiral stair, this one narrower and darker than the others.

"I must finish this alone," said Gabriel to the Lomerians as they regrouped at the stair's base.

"What?" said Malvegil. "We're in this together, Mister. I aim to see this through."

"Methinks there is only one foe left," said Gabriel. "And he is one that I must deal with alone."

"Why?" said Malvegil. "Why must it be you? It's my men that have died in this, not yours. And it's my mission. And I want to end it. And who are you to decide? You do not command here."

Gabriel paused, staring at Malvegil.

Eotrus spoke. "Torbin—"

"No," said Malvegil, gesturing for Aradon to be quiet. "Let the man speak for himself."

"I think I know who this master of the Fens is," said Gabriel. "The one the Lugron call the warlock. I want to question him. To find out what the madness we've seen here is about, and how to put an end to it. He'll not speak if we all charge in, swords and hammers swinging. If we do, he'll say nothing. But if he is who I think he is, to me alone, he may say much."

"So who is he?" said Malvegil. "A Northman?"

"No one you've ever heard of," said Gabriel. "But someone well known to me. I suggest that you head back down and put an end to those creatures in the laboratory. When it's done, I'll meet you on the stair beyond the iron door. Go, all of you," he said with a sense of urgency.

Malvegil made no move to leave, though the other men stirred, ready to follow Gabriel's direction. "I'll be waiting for you right here," said Malvegil. "And ten minutes is all you have. After that, we're coming up — swords and hammers swinging."

"Ten minutes," said Gabriel.

The men wished Gabriel well, patted him on the back, and up he went.

Alone.

As Gabriel made his way back up the stair, the Dor Lords sent Artol, Karktan, and McDuff to check on Donnelin and deal with the shamblers in the laboratory.

"We can't leave Gabe alone up there," Ob said quietly to Aradon. "I aim to follow him. I'll hang back; he won't see me, but I'll be near enough that I can help him, if help he needs."

Aradon considered that for a moment, then nodded. "Good," he said. "Up now, quick and quiet. Stay hidden unless you're needed."

***

The stair that led down to the laboratory where the shamblers were tied up, was a bloody mess.

McDuff crouched down and studied the scene for some moments from a full flight up. "Looks like the priest gave some Lugron what for," he said.

"Do you see him?" said Artol.

"He ain't moving," said McDuff. "Nothing's moving down there, best as I can see."

Artol looked behind them, concern on his face. "There could be more in the lab down there," he said, "or some could have gone up. We might have passed them, hiding in the great hall. Shadows enough in there to hide a full squadron."

The dwarf shook his head. "There's no blood trail up the steps," said McDuff. "Nobody walked through that mess and kept their shoes clean. Them Lugron aren't shifty enough to have cleaned up and gone all stealthy. Besides, we

205

used all the water in them buckets ourselves. I figure, the priest stopped all of them down there."

"What a fight that must have been," said Karktan.

"And Donnelin half dead with just one arm," said Artol. "Never knew he was that tough."

"Them what got the magic are hard to size up," said McDuff. "Never know what they're capable of. The bugger might not even be dead."

"Donnelin," said Artol. He called the priest's name three more times, pausing some moments between each, before finally, he got a response.

"Here," said a weak voice, barely audible.

They recognized Donnelin's voice and rushed down.

The carnage was worse up close. Donnelin sat leaning against the wall on the second landing up from the bottom. He was drenched in blood, head to boot. His face, bruised and cut. Wounds on his arm and legs, and across his forehead, in addition to his bloody stump. He still held his dagger firmly in hand.

Three dead Lugron lay around him on that landing, one fallen across his legs. Another three lay dead on the stairs below him. What was left of probably a half dozen more Lugron, lay in pieces at the stair's base.

Rather small pieces.

"How bad are you hurt, priest?" said McDuff.

"Not as bad as any of them," said Donnelin. Then he laughed.

***

Shouting flooded down the stairs that led up to the turret. Gabriel's shouting. With it came the smell of smoke.

Up the stairs went Aradon and Torbin, girded and ready for battle. Gabriel had been up there a long time. Maybe too long. And it sounded like he was in trouble again.

Halfway up, they met Ob, who was leaping down the steps in a panic.

"What happened?" said Aradon. "More golems?"

The gnome barred their path — stopping the charging men in their tracks.

"Don't tell him that I followed him up," said Ob, panting, his eyes wide and wild.

"What?" said Aradon. "Gabe's in trouble, move aside."

"He's alright," said Ob. "Just don't tell him that I was up there. Not this time."

"What does it matter?" said Malvegil.

"It matters!" said Ob. "There's no time to explain," he said, looking over his shoulder, as if he expected Gabriel to be right on his heels. "Swear it! Swear to me that you'll never tell him that I followed him! Both of you. Swear it!"

***

Gabriel met them at the top of the stairs, the stairwell already filling with smoke.

He carried a baby in his right arm. His left dragged a large sack filled with weapons and gear

— those things of value that Gabriel could quickly salvage.

"A child!" cried Malvegil. "Thank the gods. What of the parents? Any other captives?"

"Dining with Odin," said Gabriel, his voice harsh, a stern look on his face. He pushed past the others and kept walking down the steps.

"And the Master of the Dead?" said Malvegil, calling after him. "Was it who you thought?"

"He will trouble us no more," said Gabriel.

Fire licked the wall at the top of the stairwell. "Time for us to leave," said Gabriel. He looked back at each of the men. "Don't ask me what happened in there."

"Not ever. And tell the others not to ask me. I will not speak of it."

"What a battle that must have been," muttered Malvegil.

"It seems we'll never know," said Aradon quietly.

***

"Our work is far from done," said Malvegil to the others as they made their way to the castle's exit. "We must kill the shamblers that lurk outside. Not just enough of them for us to get clear, but all of them. Every last one. We must end this plague here and now. I'll not have more Lomerians end up like Master Gorlick."

"You'll scour the Fens?" said Gabriel.

"From end to end," said Malvegil. "However long it takes."

"Not one must be allowed to live," said Gabriel. "For even one can doom all the world."

"I'll have two companies of my finest here within two days of our return to the Dor," said Malvegil. "I have the best hounds in all Lomion. They'll sniff out the shamblers wherever they're hiding. Rest assured, none will escape us."

"You'll join us, I trust?" said Malvegil to Aradon.

"A fine-looking boy," said Aradon of the foundling that squirmed in Gabriel's arm. For some time, he'd been staring at the child. "Healthy and strong. The hand of the gods is at work in this — to save this one child. Had we arrived but a day later, mayhap, only minutes later, and this beautiful life would've been destroyed. Just as all the others that died in this place."

Aradon turned toward Malvegil. "I long for the homeward road. I will travel with you back to Dor Malvegil, of course, but then me and mine will head straight home. I've seen enough death to last me a goodly while."

Malvegil's face failed to mask his surprise.

39

THE AGE OF MYTH AND LEGEND

Just before Azrael brought his sword down, to sever Dahlia's head, a memory flashed to mind. A memory that had haunted him down through the long years.

He stood over the woman. She lay on her back, her face bloodied from where he'd hit her. Her cheek was cut open, and her nose bled. She was pretty in her way. No great beauty like Dahlia. But younger. Slimmer. Dark haired.

A sinner was she. An adulterer. A thief. A liar.

A wanton woman.

Someone to be shunned by proper folk.

She professed faith in the lord, but strayed far and wide with her misdeeds. Azathoth had forgiven her transgressions more than once. But of late, she and her sister joined a group that worshiped false idols and denounced the one true god. That last sin was unforgivable. It had sealed her fate, and that of her sister too. Azathoth himself condemned them.

"Get thee to Midgaard," said Azathoth to Azrael and Thetan, "and cleanse it of their evil. It is a sad and terrible thing, but I will suffer their pollution of my flock no longer. For them, there is only the void."

And Azrael followed those orders, just as he always followed the lord's orders. He and Thetan tracked them down, those two wanton women. They found both sisters and their idolater friends carrying on their blasphemies in a wretched hovel in the bowels of some forsaken city.

Thetan entered through the upper floor where one sister lingered; Azrael went after the other sister on the main level. When Azrael announced himself and lowered his trident to carry out the lord's justice, the idolaters did not fall to their knees and beg mercy and forgiveness. Instead, they dared raise their hands against him.

Against him! An Arkon of the lord, going about the lord's work!

Without hesitation, he put them to the sword. Their bloodied bodies heaped about the room.

The wanton woman was the last. She begged and pleaded for her life. She repented. She promised, she swore, to never sin again. To keep holy the lord's name.

Azrael paused. He gave the lord a chance to call off his vengeance. But the lord's voice did not speak to him, did not enter his mind. Therein was silence only, and his own thoughts.

There would be no pardon. No reprieve.

Azrael knew his duty. He knew what was expected of him. What the lord's justice demanded.

To kill the woman.

That was justice, for it was the lord's will. The lord's command. And he, as an Arkon, was the lord's instrument.

Yet Azrael hesitated. Killing the woman, murdering her, didn't feel right.

In fact, it felt wrong.

Terribly wrong.

But it was his duty. He was honor-bound and oath-sworn to do it. His very soul depended upon it. He could not defy the lord's will. He dare not.

He looked into the woman's eyes. He did not see evil. Instead, he saw pain. And fear. Terror. He took no pleasure in seeing her fear. That wasn't what he wanted — to be feared.

He wanted respect. He wanted love. Perhaps admiration. But fear? Never from the people. He wanted to inspire fear only in the enemies of the lord and his people. Not in common sinners. Not folks that had strayed from the lord's path. But rather, those who were truly evil. Those that made war on the lord and the lord's kingdom.

The woman before him was nothing like that. She was no threat. Not to Azrael; not to the lord, or to anyone else. She was just a weak, misguided and pitiful woman who misbehaved. Hardly more than a child was she. A rebellious child.

Did that warrant death?

Was that justice?

It was. It had to be. For the lord said so. And the lord was all knowing. All good. He was love. Such was his nature.

But still, it didn't feel right.

It wasn't right. He knew that in his heart.

But Azrael had to do it, nonetheless. He had to carry out the lord's will, just as he had done countless times before.

As the wanton woman groveled and begged for mercy, Azrael did his duty.

He raised his sword.

He took her head.

And then Thetan appeared. He looked down at the woman's corpse, and at those of the others. His face was hard. His sword was out. Azrael noticed that it was not bloodied.

"Did the sister escape you?" said Azrael.

"I found her upstairs," said Thetan. "It is done."

Azrael was confused. His eyes flicked again to Thetan's sword. Thetan noticed that glance and sheathed his blade.

"It is done," repeated Thetan, his voice resolute.

That's when Azrael knew that Thetan was a traitor. A traitor to the lord. He had not done his duty. He had spared his wanton woman. He had let her go.

He had done what Azrael could not. What Azrael didn't have the strength or the courage to do himself. And that made him ashamed.

Azrael never forgot her, the wanton woman he had murdered. Those moments in that hovel were inscribed in his mind's eye forevermore. After untold centuries he still remembered her face, her eyes, and the terrible fear that paralyzed her.

He never forgave himself.

For that and many other black deeds he'd done in Azathoth's name.

He wasn't that man anymore. An Arkon of the lord no longer. He was his own man now. He lived by his own rules. He would never feel that guilt again. That shame.

And so Azrael pulled out the short lengths of cord from his pouch — the ones they used to tie the hands and feet of the captured infected. He tied Dahlia up. Securely. Then he placed a gag over her mouth. She would not bewitch him again.

And then he thought, was it truly for mercy's sake that he spared her, or was he deluding himself?

Was it pity?

Or was it for his own selfish reasons? Did he still long for her? Did he hold out hope that he could yet cure the bloodlust and return her to normalcy? And then he'd have his chance with her?

Or, somewhere, deep down in the darkest corner of his soul, did he yet want to join with her. And devour the world? Was such madness a part of him? Was he capable of it?

Azrael could not bear to contemplate such things. He pushed those thoughts from his mind.

Then his eyes landed upon Pennebray. She still sat in the same spot as when he first entered the parlor. Still engorged to incredible extreme. How her stomach failed to burst, he had no idea.

Still unconscious was she. She'd slept through it all. The fighting. The killing. With her eyes and mouth closed, she looked so much like the little girl he'd treated in his manor those few weeks prior. Exhausted, pained, but an innocent child. He knew that wasn't true. Not any longer. He knew what she was. What she had done. What she was capable of doing.

But he didn't have the heart to kill her. To murder her. He couldn't. He wouldn't. Mercy was his to give, and he gave it. He tied her up: wrist and ankles, strong and tight. He'd take her back to Virent Hall. Dahlia too. To the dungeons with them until he decided their fate.

40

THE DEAD FENS,
THE KEEP'S TURRET

Year 1242, 4th Age
12th Year of King Tenzivel's Rule

The warlock knew he was coming. With all the noise, how could he not? Yet Gabriel used every skill he had, to quietly, silently, climb those stairs. Otherwise, he'd be inviting a well-timed arrow or dagger to the eye, the moment he reached the top.

Blood dripped from his nose. He didn't wipe it; he didn't want his hands slicker than they were. He let the blood drop to the steps — a sparse red trail that marked his passage.

The door atop the stair was ajar, but the doorway angled such that he could see nothing without stepping in. Gabriel paused there for some minutes. Listening. On a good day he could have stood there for an hour and not moved a muscle, but his head pounded; he ached all over.

Head injuries were a funny thing. Hard to tell how bad they were. He was bruised and battered, he knew that, but was it more? Time would tell. He needed to get this over with and fast, or else chance getting weaker. Maybe even passing out. And that would get him killed.

Silence ruled the room at the top of the turret, but Gabriel was certain that he heard breathing, shallow and muffled, far back from the doorway. Someone lurked within.

Gabriel stepped in, sword at the ready.

The place was a single large room, part laboratory, part living quarters. Its condition, as decayed as the great hall below.

The small laboratory area was menacing in its way, but not so gruesome as the chamber of death below. No undead writhed, croaked, or gibbered there. There were no buckets of blood; no piles of discarded limbs, no gore spread about the floor. Silence ruled there, but so did death.

A naked man, tall and thick but solid of limb, young, dark-haired, a Northman by his look, lay unmoving atop a table, tied down by leather cord at neck, chest, waist, wrists, and ankles. The man's skin was that blue shade of death and his chest neither rose nor fell. On a sideboard beside the table sat an array of instruments, tubes, and jars — the tools of torture, medicine, and of alchemy.

And off to the side, in a large, decrepit old chair set before a smoldering fireplace, sat the warlock; the master of the dead.

41

THE HOLLOW,
VIRENT HALL

Year 801, 4th Age

The long days stretched to weeks and then to months.

Azrael tirelessly worked night and day. But he found no cure for the bloodlust. No treatment. Nothing of use at all.

Two choices lay before him. Keep the infected prisoners forevermore (or until he found a cure, if ever he did), or kill them all.

The thought of murdering them was abhorrent to him — at least so long as a cure remained a possibility.

He didn't want to kill Dahlia.

He couldn't murder Pennebray.

But he couldn't keep them in his dungeon. Not forever. As the days and weeks went by, their powers grew.

They grew stronger, faster. Their minds grew clearer, more human. But still, the beasts that they had become always lay just below the service, ready to attack, to kill, whenever opportunity presented.

They'd killed more of his guards.

Some by their mind magic.

He kept all the infected bound and gagged, but he had to let them eat. Each time that he did, any guard about, even Azrael himself, was in grave danger.

He resolved to send them away. He knew it was too dangerous to keep them in The Hollow, or any other civilized place. There is an island that he knew of. Uninhabited. A place where they could live out their lives without being a threat to others. Without their contagion spreading. A place from which they could never leave. It is there that he would take them.

42

THE DEAD FENS,
THE KEEP'S TURRET

Year 1242, 4th Age
12th Year of King Tenzivel's Rule

The warlock was clad in steel plate armor, enameled a deep emerald green, dulled, dented, and chipped of age and neglect, severe of style, horned at helmet, spiked at shoulder, elbow, knee, and boot. Around his neck hung a silver chain to which was affixed an ankh to match Gabriel's. In his left hand he held a great trident. At his waist, a bejeweled leather sheath, home to an ornate dagger of Asgardian make. He looked as a king or great warlord of old, long fallen from power; brooding, mourning, waiting for death to call him home.

Gabriel's eyes widened as he stared at the figure, recognition on his face. He was right.

The warlock was Azrael the Wise.

It had to be. Still, Gabriel was surprised. And he wasn't certain. Not completely. His vision was blurry. The figure's face, what little he could see of it past the man's helmet, came into and out of focus over and again. Gabriel couldn't tell whether his injuries caused that or some sorcery that was in play.

The figure wore Azrael's armor. His accoutrements. More importantly, it wore his ankh. While he yet lived, that was the one thing that Azrael would surely never part with.

But how could Azrael have fallen to such a sorry state? Gabriel prayed that the wretch who sat before him was not his beloved friend, but rather, some usurper who plundered his long dead remains.

But in his heart, Gabriel knew the truth. He knew that the creature that sat before him was none other than Azrael the Wise. The angle at which he sat, the tilt of his head — it was he. It had to be.

"What was it that Donnelin said?" Gabriel murmured. "An ancient fiend from a bygone age?" He shook his head as if in disgust or shame. "Is that all we've come to? How far the great have fallen."

As Gabriel approached, the figure did not stir, save that his eyes opened and glowed in the gloom, reflecting the light that bounced from his armor. When he met Gabriel's steely gaze, his eyes widened in surprise, then narrowed as if he did not trust his vision.

"What a grim ghost out of the past fronts me now," said the man in a quiet voice as he eyed Gabriel, his accent foreign, strange, indeterminate.

Gabriel knew well that voice of old. Hearing it stirred memories in him. Memories of times long past. Memories of Azathoth. Memories of the great war. But he pushed those thoughts down — he had no time for them and could not afford the distraction. The man before him was Azrael the Wise. Now he was certain of it.

43

THE DEAD FENS, THE KEEP'S TURRET

Year 1242, 4th Age
12th Year of King Tenzivel's Rule

"**R**efisal," said Azrael as he glanced at the gnarled old gnome who stood in the shadows by a table filled of vials and tubes of every shape and size, "do my eyes betray me; does my mind play tricks?"

Refisal shrugged as he looked back and forth from Azrael to Gabriel.

"You wear the face of my old friend, Gabriel," said Azrael. "But surely, you cannot be him. Not here. Not now. For he must be long since dead. Little left but dust, if even that by now." Azrael leaned forward in his seat as he studied Gabriel who stood still as stone.

"Only as a ghost would Gabriel look upon me with such sour expression. A grim, bloody ghost come haunting. Begone with you," he said waving Gabriel away. "There are trolls in my keep causing mischief. I need to be ready. I need to put them down. I've no time for restless spirits; not today of all days. Haunt me no more, spectre. Begone." He tightly closed his eyes for several moments. When he opened them, Gabriel was still there.

Azrael turned again to Refisal. "You do see him, don't you? He is real, isn't he?"

"I see him, Master," said Refisal. "A tall knight clad in ornate armor of archaic design. His face, bloodied and bruised. His armor, battered and blood strewn; his hair, matted with it. But whether he is a mortal man, vengeful spirit, or something else, I cannot say."

Azrael looked surprised. "What a crafty ghost you be, to appear to us both. Or else a lookalike or a doppleganger, mayhap?"

"No, not that. A shade of the past is all you are; a spectre of old memory you be, for I am the last of the great Arkons of the lord. The last of the Eternals. All gone but me. All the great ones. Gone."

"Alone I dwell in this grand castle on a hill," said Azrael. "Alone in my shame, and guilt, and long regret. Alone in my labors, save for the gnome and what few servants yet remain. Why do you haunt me? Why trouble me now, spectre, in my hour of triumph? Even on this day of days can you give me no peace? Speak now or get you gone."

Gabriel drew closer, slowly, his steps stiff and uncharacteristically uncertain.

Azrael removed his helmet, as if to see and be seen, the better. At first glance, Azrael's face was gaunt, hollow and sunken, almost akin to the shambling dead. A shadow of his former self. But on closer view, his aspect was still regal and strong, his features still handsome. He looked neither young, nor old, just very tired and sad.

He stood, trident held at his side. Tall was he, a match to Gabriel.

"No warm greetings do you offer your old friend, shade of Gabriel?" said Azrael. "No wisdom? No threats or warnings? No dire portents? No words at all?"

Gabriel said nothing.

"For Azathoth's sake, can't you at least groan and rattle your chains?"

"No?" Azrael glanced over at Refisal again. The gnome shrugged but offered no council. "You were a far better man than you are a ghost," said Azrael. "Taciturn even then, but not a mute. Keep your silence if you wish."

"Mayhap you are here for humbler purpose," said Azrael. "Not to speak, but to listen — which is just as well, because I have news to tell. Good news. Great news. And tell someone of it I must — as yet, only the gnome and I know the truth."

"The Lugron—" said Refisal.

"The Lugron have ears but they do not hear," said Azrael. "They have eyes, but they do not see. Fools they are. Useful in their way, like a hammer or a saw. But poor companions do they make. Foolish as children. They need to be led. And controlled. And kept out of trouble. As you well know, I've little interest or stomach for any of that."

"Brace yourself, shade of Gabriel, for my news is great, but not grave. Of all the years, the centuries, the eons, that I've labored, today, this very day, is my day of success. My long sought victory. My prayed for solace."

"Can you believe it? I knew this day would come, if only I persevered, so I have done nothing but. But now that the day is here, even I can't believe it. Not even now, though the truth of it lay before me."

Refisal opened his mouth to speak, but Azrael's pointed palm checked him. "It's true that I have been wrong before," he said looking first to Refisal and then to Gabriel. "There have been setbacks. Failures. Grave disappointments. But not this time. This time I have found it." His eyes darted back and forth as if to spy out unseen eavesdroppers. "Spectre," he said, his voice now a whisper, "I have discovered the cure."

"The cure.

"This very day. The cure for the great plague."

Refisal nodded and beamed with pride.

Gabriel stood stoic and silent, sword in hand. He did not move a hair. He did not even blink.

"No reaction?" said Azrael. "Not even to that? A grim ghost, indeed. Refisal, perhaps we're both befuddled. Even now I don't trust my eyes. I don't know whether what stands before me is man or figment." Azrael's brow furrowed and he put a hand to his forehead as if in pain.

"I don't get enough sleep, you see. I can't sleep for days on end. And then I see things. Terrible things. But good things too. Things that aren't there, but seem real. It's a wonder I've kept up my work through that, all these years. Duty carries me on, Gabriel. That's what it is, you know. And obligation. Repentance. Guilt. Poor reasons for carrying on, but they serve."

Azrael stepped closer to Gabriel, his eyes narrowing. "You're nothing like the man you once were. Though who am I to speak?" he said with a chuckle. Frustration crept over Azrael's face. "Why have you come here if you will not speak a word to me? Speak my name at least, won't you, for Azathoth's sake? It has been so long since I have heard it. Do you not know me? Have I changed so much?"

"I knew you," said Gabriel, his voice calm, and no louder than needed for the man to hear him. "I knew Azrael."

"Your voice is as I remember," said Azrael. "Though until I heard it just now, I could not have described it. It has been too long. The years have gotten away from us."

"I have been haunted before," said Azrael. "Many times. Plagued by visions. Memories. Even ghosts. More often than not, those come from within," he said as he pointed to his head. "But you are different. You seem . . . solid. Are you real? And here, in my castle? Or are you naught but a figment? Or a memory? Tell me true. I must know. I must."

"I am real," said Gabriel.

"You hear him, don't you?" he said to Refisal.

"He is real," said the gnome, "standing before us, or else some sorcery confounds us both. Go carefully, Master."

Azrael smiled, a long, sincere smile. "Two wonders, unimaginable, in a single day." He slapped his thigh, as if to check whether he was awake or dreaming. "The long elusive cure at last found, and you, my dear, dear friend – the lord's

Arkon Gabriel – here before me, in my own humble abode, my little castle on the great green hillside. How can it be? How can it be? Such coincidence be not possible." Azrael's eyes grew watery. "What has brought you here?"

Gabriel said nothing further. He merely stared at Azrael.

"No matter," said Azrael. "You are here and that is what's important. We must celebrate. A party. No, a grand ball. All the townsfolk will come."

"But Master,—" said Refisal.

Azrael's hand went up and the gnome went silent. Azrael's voice and expression grew serious again. "I have atoned for our sins, Gabriel. For our betrayal. It is here," he said, carefully grasping a crystal flask filled with a murky greenish blue fluid that he plucked from a table nearby. "The cure."

44

THE DEAD FENS, THE KEEP'S TURRET

Year 1242, 4th Age
12th Year of King Tenzivel's Rule

"**H**e will never die now," said Azrael, gesturing toward the man on the table. The man that looked dead.

"I gave the last subject too large a dose and it killed him, the poor soul." Azrael vigorously shook his head and tightly closed his eyes for a moment. "There I go again. Thinking of them as people." He lowered his voice to a whisper, as if he spoke only to himself. "I can't do that. I must not do that. They're subjects, test subjects, nothing more. I have to remind myself of that," he said, now speaking to Gabriel again.

"I have to make it sink in. If not, I cannot go on. I could not do what needs to be done. The work. It's all important. All Midgaard depends on the results. Sacrifices must be made. The ends, Gabriel. The ends sometimes justify the means. At least in extreme cases like this. Don't they? Tell me true. I'm doing the right thing, aren't I?"

"You think it right for the dead to walk?" said Gabriel.

Azrael looked horrified. "Failures," he said loudly, his voice breaking up. "In science, there are always failures, mistakes. Dead ends. It's terrible, but it is the nature of—"

"They're out there hunting men," shouted Gabriel as a wave of dizziness crept over him. A concussion for certain. He was afraid of that.

"You don't understand," said Azrael. "I had them safely contained where they couldn't harm anyone. But they were going to drown. A wall collapsed in the basement and water rushed in. Foul smelling stuff — a sewerage pipe must have burst in the street. No one came to fix it — the weekend, you know. Azathoth forbid, anyone dare work on the weekend. The lazy sots."

"I plan to have sharp words with the mayor about it. Mark my words, the town will pay restitution for the damages. Paid in full. You'll see. The mayor has no wish to risk my ire."

"Still, I don't know how the wall fell. It shouldn't have happened. The servants keep up the castle so well. Everything minded and mended; all functioning—"

"It's a ruin," said Gabriel. "Open your eyes, man. It's a ruin. There is no town, no servants. You're out of your—"

"I couldn't let them drown down there," said Azrael. "I knew that once I perfected the cure, I could save them, heal them, bring them back. But I had to keep them safe until then. I had no choice but to let them out of their cells. I had to give them a chance. They deserved that, didn't they? A chance?"

Gabriel made no response save to shake his head.

"It must have been the right thing to do," said Azrael. "All the subjects. What I did. What I had to do; to them. And all that I've endured, not that I matter. I stopped mattering a long time ago, if ever I mattered at all, so let's not make this about me. I am but the instrument of our will. The will of the Eternals. To accomplish the holy purpose to which we set out at the very beginning, all those ages ago. I've stayed true to that purpose — the duty assigned to me. I've persevered. I've done my penance, Gabriel. I have. Believe me, I have."

"But it doesn't matter now," said Azrael. "None of it matters any more. Not after today. Not after the success. I adjusted the latest subject's dosage far down and accounted for size and weight and age. I won't bore you with the technical details. The formulations. They are complicated."

"No offense, but you never had a head for such things, so you wouldn't grasp it anyway. But suffice to say, for now at least, that it worked. The final breakthrough. Complete success."

"At long, long last. It really worked," he said shaking his head, as if he didn't really believe it himself. "Untold years of experimentation and now it's done. It's over."

His eyes locked on Gabriel's. "I had to do things, Gabriel," he said, his face distorting with anguish, tears flowing down his cheeks. "Terrible things. Unspeakable things." A look of suspicion came over Azrael's face. "Did you know that I would? That I was capable of such things? Is that why this task fell to me?"

Gabriel shook his head. It felt like it weighed a hundred pounds. His vision was blurry, his balance was off. He was thinking about puking. Stinking concussion.

"No, of course not," said Azrael. "What was I thinking? I don't know. I lost myself, Gabriel. My standards. I had to. I had to forget who I was; who we are. I had to forget all that we stood for. I had to toss aside my values, my conscience, everything. All to arrive at this day."

"To be here now."

"To hold this in my hand," he said as he held the crystal flask up before his face. "To stand triumphant. It's over at last. The world's suffering is over. And my toils are done; save to make more of this."

"A lot more. Enough for everyone. I'm tired, so tired, but I will do it. I will not rest until the great plague is but a bad memory."

"Don't you see, Gabriel? He's just like us now," he said, looking and gesturing again toward the body on the table. "He's free of the plague. He will never die. He will live forever as was always meant to be. He is cured." Azrael lowered his chin to his chest, put his hand over his face, and wept. "He is cured. I did it. Finally. I cured him. I have saved the world."

45

THE DEAD FENS, THE KEEP'S TURRET

Year 1242, 4th Age
12th Year of King Tenzivel's Rule

Gabriel looked over at the man who lay motionless on the table, his chest unmoving. He wasn't breathing. Gabriel moved to his side, never taking his eyes from Azrael, who stood there weeping, paying Gabriel no heed. Gabriel felt for the man's pulse at wrist and neck and put a hand to his chest. He found no spark of life; only cold dead flesh. Dead for a day at least. The man's body was undamaged, save for small puncture marks and a trickle of dried blood on his forearm.

"Surely we shall be forgiven now," said Azrael as Gabriel walked toward him. "With this miracle in hand," he said of the flask's contents, "and all the long years that have passed, surely the lord Azathoth will give us another chance. Won't he?"

Gabriel opened his mouth, ready to speak, but suddenly, Azrael started, and staggered back, one step, and then another. "Has the lord sent you to bring me home? Back to Vaedon? Is that why you're here? It must be. Oh, dear lord, thank you. Thank you," he said as he fell to his knees before Gabriel, sobbing.

"Terrible, terrible deeds," said Azrael as he shook his head, his eyes downcast.

"That is all over now, brother," said Gabriel softly.

"Yes. Yes, all over now. I had to find the cure. My duty. My purpose. I had to do what I did, for the good of all, even if it damned my soul for all eternity. I had to do it. You understand, don't you? We all had our labors, you had yours, and this was the one that fell to me. My job, my burden."

Gabriel nodded as Azrael looked up. "Aye, it was. A terrible burden."

"What happens to me now doesn't matter," said Azrael. "I will give myself over to the lord's justice. I am nothing. Just one old man. One pitiful wretch. A traitor to my god. A man seeking naught but redemption — and the cure. And I found it — the cure at least. I have saved mankind, Gabriel. I have made Midgaard whole again — or I will have, once this cure is dispensed to all. I have paid our debt," he said looking up to Gabriel who only gave back a hard, piercing gaze.

"Had you come only yesterday, I would have told you that I regretted it all. All the horrors," he said, shaking his head, anguish in his voice. "All to no avail. Such suffering. Such black deeds. And for naught. All for naught. But today, everything is different."

"This changes everything," he said, indicating the vial. "Now I know that it was worth it. It was a price that needed to be payed — in blood, and lives, and the black stain upon my immortal soul. It was a burden that I needed to bear."

234

"But you know that. You must. Surely, your arrival be no coincidence, no happenstance. The lord sent you to me. To bring me before him. But will it be in triumph or in chains, brother? I will go willingly with you, either way. I will raise no hand against you and accept my fate, whatever it be. Whatever the lord has decreed. Tell me true, brother. Are you here to carry me home? Tell me," he said weeping.

"Yes, brother," said Gabriel as he moved to Azrael's side. Gabriel gently placed his hand on Azrael's shoulder, and then placed his palm against Azrael's cheek. "I have come to send you home."

For the first time in a long time, Azrael looked content. For that instant, he felt at peace. He turned toward Refisal and pointed at him. "We must take Refisal too. Without his help, I could never have found the cure. He can come with us? Say that it will be so."

Gabriel looked to where Azrael pointed, just as he had several times during their conversation.

There was no one there. No gnome called Refisal; no one at all.

"Aye," said Gabriel. "It will be so."

THE DEAD FENS,
THE KEEP'S TURRET

Year 1242, 4th Age
12th Year of King Tenzivel's Rule

Azrael looked up at Gabriel, his cheeks wet.

His smile turned to shock just as Gabriel's sword arced into his neck.

Azrael's head flew from his body and rolled across the room. A fountain of blood sprang up; some splashed across Gabriel's tunic and cheek. The body fell forward, the crystal vial still tightly clutched within Azrael's hand. Gabriel watched it fall as if in slow motion. When Azrael's corpse hit the floor, the vial shattered and loosed its strange contents forevermore.

Gabriel was thankful that he didn't have to destroy that vial himself. He didn't want to touch the evil stuff. The thought of all the suffering it had caused made him want to retch. At least the man on the table was the last victim. The last victim of the mad warlock of the Dead Fens.

Gabriel dropped to one knee before his old friend's body, as much from pain and exhaustion as from grief. He could hardly believe he had just killed him. He felt a lump in his throat; his heart was racing. It didn't feel real. It didn't feel right.

Was it mercy, the killing? Or was it murder? Was it justice?

It didn't matter in the end. It had to be done and so Gabriel did it. There was no curing Azrael's mind. He was too far gone. And far too dangerous to be left to his own devices. What other option did he have? Imprison Azrael forever? If he even could.

No doubt, he'd escape, however sound the prison. Mad or not, Azrael was highly skilled, highly intelligent, and very resourceful.

He had to die.

It was the only way.

Or so Gabriel told himself.

"How came you to this sorry state, brother?" whispered Gabriel. "You who were ever so wise and true and brave. How came you to this foul end? What madness took you?"

After a brief time, Gabriel turned aside and quickly searched through Azrael's possessions. He would take the ankh, of course, but also any other relics or devices of mystic power. Gabriel would not have such fall into the hands of random looters that happened by.

First, he picked up Azrael's ankh, which dripped with its master's blood. Gabriel held it up by its chain and studied it, taking care not to touch it with his bare hands. Though of similar size, that ankh was lighter and less battered than his, its limbs straighter and smoother. Gabriel wondered if any man ever possessed two such powerful relics.

He doubted it.

One was enough for any man — even an Eternal.

But now he had two.

He carefully stowed it in his waist pouch. Before he dare use it, he'd need to study it at length to unlock its mysteries and avoid its dangers, for each ankh was different in its way. And each was dangerous. Terribly dangerous. He would make good use of it.

The moment Gabriel picked up Azrael's trident, he felt its mystic power — a strange sensation: a vibration that tickled his fingers, an electricity that coursed up and down his arms. It made the thing uncomfortable to hold, though he gritted his teeth and withstood it. Gabriel suspected it was the weapon's wood haft that held its power — the trident of steel that capped it merely an accoutrement that concealed its true nature and extended its use.

So too did Gabriel find an assortment of personal affects, and a shield beside Azrael's chair — a thing of ornate make and expert craftsmanship, long now in disrepair.

He held one volume of Azrael's journals in his hand and leafed through it. There was a whole shelf of them: journals, logs, ledgers, records. Everything about Azrael's experiments. His thoughts. His opinions. His feelings. Theories. Everything. Thousands of pages. Some volumes were recent. Some were old. Others were ancient. Gabriel's first impulse was to scoop them all up and take them with him — to read them, to learn what had happened to his friend. To understand what brought him to that pitiful state.

And perhaps, to learn something that could truly lead to a cure for the plague.

But he didn't have Azrael's skill, his patience, or his meticulousness. Perhaps no one did. If Azrael couldn't find the cure after so many years, it was likely that no one could.

Gabriel told himself that the man that he knew, that he loved as a brother, did not die that day: did not die at his hands.

He was long since dead.

The mad shell that remained was unworthy of Azrael's legacy. It was a mercy that Gabriel put him down.

A mercy.

Or so he tried to convince himself.

"The ravings of a madman," muttered Gabriel as he perused one volume of rambling notes. "Best they go unread. And the man that you once were, be remembered." He dropped the journal, left the others on the shelves.

"Forgive me, brother," said Gabriel, his voice quaking, "for what I had to do. I will not forget you. I will not forget your valor the day we stood together against Azathoth — the day we set Midgaard free. I will not forget your deeds at R'yleh; your battles with Balthazar, and with the great wyrm, and all the rest."

"You should have a grand funeral — a memorial fit for a king of kings; thousands in attendance, weeping and wailing at your loss; stories and songs of your deeds told all the month long. A statue erected in the great square. All that and more."

"But there is only me. No one else remembers. Only me. That isn't much. It's not what you deserve, but it's something at least. For as long as I walk Midgaard, for as long as life remains in me, Azrael the Wise will be remembered."

Gabriel poured a large flask of lamp oil over Azrael's corpse. His hand shook as he dropped a burning lantern to set the oil ablaze. He emptied several other flasks of oil about the room and set them alight, one and all.

As he turned to leave, Gabriel heard a cry. A cry from within the room.

The cry of a child.

THE DEAD FENS, THE KEEP'S TURRET

Year 1242, 4th Age
12th Year of King Tenzivel's Rule

Gabriel spun about. At first he didn't know if the cry he heard was real. Was his mind playing tricks? His head was still pounding, still dizzy. Maybe it was a hallucination?

But the sound continued. It grew louder even as the flames grew higher about him and the smoke thicker. Gabriel raced to where the dead man lay upon the table and searched about, for the sound came from there. Just beyond the table, on the floor, amid a thick pile of blankets, he found the source of the cries.

A baby.

A human child. A Volsung by the look of it, not more than a few months old. It was alive and seemingly well, concealed amongst the blankets.

Gabriel's eyes widened when he saw the puncture wound in the baby's arm. His mouth dropped open as he realized the terrible truth.

It was not the dead man that Azrael had cured.

It was the baby. The whole time, he was talking about the baby.

The pile of blankets was in plain sight from where Azrael had stood by his chair, the child sleeping peacefully within it. But the babe was hidden from Gabriel's view throughout their conversation. He never saw it stir, nor heard it cry. If his head hadn't been so foggy, surely he would have noticed it.

"Arrgh!" Gabriel roared.

"Arrgh! Dammit!" Gabriel snatched up the child and held him protectively to his chest. He ran to Azrael's corpse and looked for the crystal vial. Its remnants were already gone, consumed by flame, its contents lost forever — and if Azrael spoke true, the cure for the great plague lost with it.

"Arrgh!"

Gabriel went for the journals, but it was too late.

All aflame.

Fully engulfed.

No chance to salvage them. No chance to ever reproduce Azrael's experiments.

"Arrgh!"

THE DEAD FENS,
THE KEEP'S TURRET

Year 1242, 4th Age
12th Year of King Tenzivel's Rule

A rush of air swept through Azrael's burning hall after Gabriel retreated down the steps carrying the child. A lithe figure clad in green and yellow stepped through the flames and knelt beside Azrael's body. Midgaard's face was filled of anguish, her cheeks wet.

A mere wave of her hand extinguished the flames that devoured Azrael's body and held back the fire for several yards in all directions. With the slightest gesture of her finger, Azrael's severed head rose into the air of its own accord and moved to its proper place against his neck.

Midgaard averted her eyes; she could not bear to look at the ruin that was Azrael's corpse. Sobbing, she moved her hand slowly over his charred face, already unrecognizable, and as she did, his face returned to its normal aspect, the burns gone, his skin restored, his head once again attached to his neck — not even a scar left behind. Her hand continued across his chest and the remainder of his body, and restored it just the same. Then she lifted Azrael across her lap as if he was as light as a child, and held him close against her breast, her hand stroking his forehead and hair.

"Oh, how touching," said a gravelly voice from nearby. "It almost makes me want to weep. Or to vomit."

Startled, Midgaard looked up.

"Why mourn him, when you can bring him back?" said the voice. "You have the power."

Refisal stepped through the flames and approached her, though the flames did him no harm. It was he that spoke.

Midgaard's face hardened. She pointed her palm outward and a transparent sphere of protective energy appeared around her, she and Azrael at its center.

"Fear me, do you?" said Refisal. Then he laughed, a smug, satisfied laugh. "Well that you should. But I've told you before that I'm saving you for last. If not, who would appreciate my efforts, my victories? Without an audience, I'm just playing to myself. That's not nearly as much fun. But never fear, when the time comes, and it will come, I have grand plans for your demise."

"So are you here to gloat over your victory?" said Midgaard. "Or to take pleasure in my grief? Which pettiness is it this time, creature?"

"Surely you don't think this is my victory?" said Refisal. "It's yours, my dear. I'm here to congratulate you; though as usual you did nothing to earn it. As for your grief, it's laughable. Embarrassing. To cry over a petty creature such as that? A talking ape."

"For me," said Refisal, "these events are an annoying loss. They will delay my plans. Even

244

now, Gabriel and his followers are putting the infected to the sword. They'll hunt the rest down. All of them. And that will stop the spread of the contagion. Worse, my most accomplished necromancer is dead," he said pointing to Azrael's corpse.

"Azrael is mine," said Midgaard. "Not yours."

"Dear lady," said Refisal, a smile forming on his face. "He hasn't been yours in a very long time."

Midgaard narrowed her eyes. "You will not win."

Refisal shook his head and rolled his eyes. "What a silly, self-deluding thing you are."

"I always win," he said.

"I make the rules, so how could I not?"

"My champions—" said Midgaard.

"Fall one by one," said Refisal. "In the end, I will take them all from you. You will stand alone."

"Some are beyond your corruption," said Midgaard. "Mithron will stop you. Or Gabriel. Or one of the others. And Thetan will destroy you — he'll rip your heart from your chest and crush it before your eyes."

"Ha!" went Refisal. "You give your toys far too much credit. In the end, if I cannot turn them, trick them, or bend them to my will, I will kill them. One and all."

"But not yet," said Refisal. "Not so quick. Not until I tire of them. They yet amuse me."

"The Old Ones will never have this world," said Midgaard. "My children will stop you, just as Gabriel did today."

"To avoid destruction, your puny minions must stop me at every turn," said Refisal. "I need prevail only once."

"Get you gone," said Midgaard. "Let me grieve in peace."

"You do that," said Refisal. "Grow accustomed to it. For in time, you will know nothing but grief."

49

THE DEAD FENS, ON THE WAY BACK TO DOR MALVEGIL

**Year 1242, 4th Age
12th Year of King Tenzivel's Rule**

"You've ordered us home," said Gabriel. "Why? There's important work left to do. The Fens must be scoured from end to end. Not one of the shamblers can be allowed to live."

"The Malvegils are more than capable," said Aradon. "We're going home."

"Why?"

Before he answered, Aradon looked around to make certain that no one was close enough to hear. "I'm keeping the child. The foundling."

Gabriel didn't look surprised. "To what end?" he said.

"I have no heir."

"What reason did you give Malvegil for our leaving?"

"I told him that Eleanor is heavy with child. That I've been away too long already and probably missed its birth. That we hoped to surprise him with the child on our next visit."

"His first nephew. He'll travel north to see him and his sister."

"Of course he will," said Aradon. "But not until the Fens campaign is done. Duty first — at least with something as serious as the shamblers."

"And when he visits, you'll pass the foundling off as your own."

"Better to have an illegitimate child," said Gabriel, "than one not of your own blood."

"No one will know he's not of my blood," said Aradon. "Save for you. And Talbon, Donnelin, Ob, and Artol." Then Aradon's voice slowed, his statement a command. "None of you will ever speak of it."

"And if the Malvegils ask after the foundling?"

"We're giving the child to a barren family from the Dor. We're keeping it quiet out of respect for them. It won't even be a lie."

"Others will suspect," said Gabriel. "They'd have noticed that Eleanor was not showing these past months."

"It was a long, cold winter. We had few visitors, and Eleanor was well covered in winter clothes when we did."

"Some of the servants will know the truth."

"Silver is a powerful persuader where loyalty and good judgment alone prove insufficient."

"Knowing you," said Gabriel, "I bet you've already chosen a name for him."

"I have," said Aradon. "We'll call the boy, Claradon, after Eleanor's father."

"He's not truly a foundling," said Gabriel. "He has a family."

"They are dead."

"Those that were with him on the ship are dead," said Gabriel. "No doubt, there are others.

It may be that his mother or father, or even both, were not on the boat with him. We may be able to trace them through the name of the ship."

"We'll say that we tried and failed," said Aradon. "Fate took the boy from whatever family he had. Our sweat and blood saved him. The child is mine now. I've claimed him."

"It's not right."

"I will not lose Eleanor. This child will change everything for us. I will not pass up this chance. And I will not debate it further."

"The boy may have the illness," said Gabriel.

"It has been a week. He is healthy."

"He may be a carrier," said Gabriel. "A single scratch or bite or even a kiss from him may infect another."

"I don't believe that," said Aradon. "We've seen no other carriers. The wet nurse suffers no ill affects. The boy is healthy. The boy is mine. My son. I have claimed him and that is the end of it. He will be my heir."

"This is a mistake—"

"It's my decision, and it's made," said Aradon. "Do not bring it up again. Do not speak of this matter again. Not with anyone. Not ever."

50

DOR MALVEGIL

Year 1242, 4th Age
12th Year of King Tenzivel's Rule

When Lord Malvegil's longship entered Dor Malvegil's harbor, it flew the red and black — the flag of death — below House Malvegil's stately banner, and red and black smoke rose from censers at both fore and aft. All who saw those signs knew what they meant — that some of the longship's passengers or crew had not returned alive.

Word spread. The townsfolk ran out to see — for they all knew that the great lords of the Malvegils and the Eotrus were themselves on that expedition. If either of them had fallen, they needed to know. Hundreds gathered before the ship even reached its berth.

The two lords stood shoulder to shoulder at the fore as the ship came in, so that all could see them, and know that they were alive, and that they were real — that neither they nor the ship were ghosts or figments come up the river with the mist. The lords' surviving lieutenants, famous men all, lined the rails to either side, so that they too could be seen. Even Brother Donnelin was there, despite his grievous wounds; Par Talbon too, though others supported them both.

Many folk cheered and called his name when they saw Lord Malvegil, much beloved of his people.

Soon came the calls for the others.

"Where be the wizard?" cried members of the crowd.

"Where be the Pict?" they shouted.

Tradition demanded that any man whose name or title was called must step forward and show themselves to the people. If they didn't, it could mean only one thing.

That they were dead.

All that mattered then, was the manner of their deaths. Did they fall as warriors, in battle with the enemy, earning them a coveted place in Valhalla; did they die by accident or illness; or did they pass as cowards, in dishonor and shame?

Torbin Malvegil stepped off the longship first; Aradon Eotrus, a step behind. The others followed after them.

A hush came over the crowd even as more and more folk joined their ranks.

Lord Malvegil raised his hands to focus their attention and signal quiet.

The Angel of Death was there — a tall but stooped, lanky fellow that was already ancient when Torbin was a boy. A necklace of bones was about his neck and a thurible that spewed black smoke in his hand. Two old war dogs sat at his feet.

Par Rorbit's wife was there — right up front, as close to Torbin as was anyone. Her eyes were watery, her face, solemn. Her husband was nowhere to be seen. She knew what that meant. She knew that he was dead.

"Three of our warriors fell in the Dead Fens," said Malvegil in loud voice, "defending our lands against a Lugron incursion from the east. Master Gorlick the Bold, our Weapons Master, has fallen; Par Rorbit, our House Wizard has fallen; and Red Tybor the Pict, our Master Scout has fallen. They died as warriors. As heroes. We will never forget their names. We will never forget their deeds. And they will remember us when they drink beside Odin in his great hall in Valhalla."

DOR MALVEGIL

Year 1242, 4th Age
12th Year of King Tenzivel's Rule

Lady Landolyn stood alone in the moonlight at the balustrade of Dor Malvegil's fourth floor balcony, wine goblet in hand, looking down at the lights of the town far below.

Sir Gabriel silently approached her from behind.

She wore an alluring perfume unknown to him. And an even more alluring dress that hugged curves possible only on a woman touched with elven blood. She turned as he neared.

"You move quietly, sir."

Gabriel was surprised that she heard him approach at all. Or was it mere chance that she turned at that moment? If so, she was skilled at concealing her reactions for she didn't seem at all surprised to see him.

"Few could approach me undetected," she said.

"It's well known that you have the sight," said Gabriel, though he knew that was not how she detected him. Prescience, for all its wonder, did not enhance one's hearing, nor did it provide any other means of detecting things. It merely gave one the power to foresee certain future events, although usually unreliably. Beyond prescience, she had magic, that one, or so he believed. Or maybe just really good hearing.

She smiled. "I thought you'd be in the drawing room with Torbin and the others, talking and drinking the night away."

"I wasn't invited. Your husband doesn't like me much."

She looked confused for a moment, then nodded knowingly. "Lords don't care for men of consequence who aren't lords themselves. They see them as a threat." She took a sip of wine. "Are you a threat, Sir Gabriel?"

"Are you?" he said pointedly.

She paused, staring at him before responding, her expression, serious. "Only to those who mean my family harm."

"Does Castellan Mordel mean your family harm?"

She looked surprised. "I don't follow your meaning. Mordel has served faithfully as House Malvegil's Castellan for over thirty years."

"Yet your husband offered Ob his position. Why would you seek to displace a man so loyal?"

Gabriel detected a hint of annoyance on her face and in her voice. "Mordel is old. His mind is not as sharp as it once was."

"He runs the House well," said Gabriel. "Everything seems quite in order."

"I've no complaints," said Landolyn.

"But he doesn't offer the good council he once did," said Gabriel. "Council your husband relied on."

"He does his best."

"Your husband is fortunate to have your good counsel. I would think that what you offer more than supplements any edge that Mordel has lost. There seems little need here for the gnome."

"I agree," said Lady Landolyn nodding. "As far as I'm concerned, we've no need of him at all. He hasn't accepted, has he?"

"Not yet," said Gabriel. "But I fear that he might. Your husband is very persuasive, which is why I've sought you out. Dor Eotrus needs Ob — his knowledge, his skills, his experience. He knows the north better than any man in the House. Those northern skills are of limited use here, so far from the mountains. He's much more valuable to the Eotrus than he ever would be to the Malvegils."

"And yet even now my husband works to convince him to accept the position, no doubt. How do we stop this?"

"We may not be able to," said Gabriel. "The gnome is his own man. He will not listen to me. But your husband listens to you. No doubt you could persuade him to withdraw his offer."

"No doubt I could," said Landolyn. "I will speak to him on this at once."

"I was hoping that you would," said Gabriel. "For, as I said, to lose Ob would be a great blow to the Eotrus, though less so than the losses your House has suffered."

Lady Landolyn nodded and looked down, her voice, solemn. "Par Rorbit's loss is a great sorrow. He was one of the most accomplished wizards in the realm and a good friend to my husband these many years. We will miss him dearly."

"And Sir Gorlick too, of course," said Gabriel. "And Red Tybor — your House Weapons Master and Master Scout."

She nodded, a sad expression on her face. "Those are losses from which we will not soon recover. Painful losses. I grieve for their families."

"And your House Cleric passed but a year ago," said Gabriel. "Did he not?"

"Such men are hard to replace," said Lady Landolyn.

"At least your husband returned unscathed, thank the gods," said Gabriel.

"Indeed," she said. Her eyes narrowed as she looked at him.

"But that was surely no surprise to you," said Gabriel. "With your powers, with your second sight, you must have known that he would return, didn't you?"

"I knew that his time on Midgaard was not at its end."

"It's a pity that you didn't see Rorbit's end coming. Or Gorlick's, or Red Tybor's. Men your husband relied on above all others. If you had, surely would have forewarned them."

Her face went pale. "I cannot see all men's futures."

"But I trust that you can see the folly of sending only six Malvegils and six Eotrus into that swamp? It was only on your word that the party was limited to twelve. We would have brought a large force otherwise. And if we had, those men wouldn't be dead."

"You don't know that. In any case, other soldiers would have been killed. Maybe more than just those three."

"But your husband's chief advisers wouldn't all be dead. Perhaps one of them, but not two, and certainly not all three."

"I see now why my husband doesn't like you," said Lady Landolyn, her voice dangerous. "I am beginning to dislike you too."

"Then let me speak all the plainer," said Gabriel. "So that we have no misunderstandings between us. You manipulated things so that only that small group went into the Fens because you wanted Malvegil's advisers dead. With them gone, and your castellan befuddled, the great lord of the Malvegils would turn to you, and you alone, for counsel. He'd have to, for he'd have no one else. Only you. Oh, and the dwarf, McDuff. I wonder what terrible fate awaits him? And if Malvegil ever sought to replace the men lost, you'd have a hand in their choosing. More than a hand, I expect."

"You weave a fanciful tale, sir knight," said Lady Landolyn sharply. "A penchant for drama and fiction do you have. Or else a troubled mind. Perhaps you'd do well to confine your attacks to the battlefield. Here you are out of your element, out of line, and outmatched. I could have you tossed in the dungeon for your accusations. Your insults."

"Think you could, do you?" said Gabriel with a fake smile. "Steer clear of the Eotrus, madam," he said sternly. "Involve them not in any plots or ploys, schemes or trickery. Not now. Not ever."

257

"How dare you—"

"You are more than you seem," said Gabriel. "That is plain to me. That I am more than I seem should be as plain to you. If you leave the Eotrus be, you and I will have no quarrel. But if you meddle in their affairs, or do them any harm, I promise you—"

"You'll do what? Who in Helheim do you think you are, speaking to me like—?"

Her words cut off as she was lifted into the air by forces unknown. Her throat compressed as if strangled by unseen hands; her feet dangled inches above the floor. Shock and pain filled her face.

She could not speak. She could not breathe. Her wine goblet tumbled to the floor and shattered. Her hands went to her throat in attempt to dislodge whatever held her, but her fingers found no purchase, nothing to dislodge.

Higher did she rise. Above the balustrade now and outward, over the edge. If she fell, she'd plummet hundreds of feet to her death.

Gabriel stood before her. His face, hard as stone. His expression, cold as the deep mountains. "You asked, who I am," he said. "I'm someone that even monsters fear." He paused, letting those words sink in.

"Dare not cross me, witch woman. Dare not cross the Eotrus. If you do, your corpse will never be found."

And then the unseen force released her and Landolyn fell.

Somehow, she landed on the balcony, having only fallen a foot or two. But she was barely conscious from lack of air. She looked up, blinking through watery eyes as she tried to catch her breath. But she was alone on the balcony. Gabriel was gone.

52

LOMION CITY, HOUSE ALDER

Year 1242, 4th Age
12th Year of King Tenzivel's Rule

Mother Alder knocked, but did not pause as she entered her brother's study. His chainmail shirt and greaves still on, Rom reclined in the big plush chair, his feet up, a tumbler in hand. A half empty bottle of raspen brandy sat beside him. The rest of his armor, and all his weapons and gear, lay strewn about the floor. His face was stoic. He glanced at his sister, expressionless, but then looked away, his jaw set.

Mother Alder knew at once that it was bad. Very bad. Rom had been away for nearly a month — but didn't even greet her. Not even a smile. That wasn't like him. And there he was, home only minutes, yet already overindulging in expensive brandy and mistreating his gear — the first, he rarely did; the second, never.

Mother Alder felt a lump develop in her throat. She didn't want to hear what had happened. She didn't want to face it. Better to turn and run. To forget Rom was home and go back to hoping that everything would be alright. But what use was pretending? One look at his face, at that room, and she knew. Things would never be alright again.

She had to be strong for him and the family. She couldn't show any sign of weakness. She wouldn't. Not ever. So it didn't matter how hard it was, she had to hear it all. She had to know the truth, whatever it was.

Her hands shook as she poured a brandy for herself; she focused her thoughts and tightened her grip to put a stop to the shaking. She wasn't successful, but Rom didn't seem to notice. He wouldn't say anything even if he did. A good brother. Respectful. He knew his place.

They sat in silence for several minutes until she couldn't stand it any longer. "Tell me," she said, her voice hoarse and quiet as a whisper; she barely recognized it. She barely got the words out.

"There will be no ransom demands," said Rom, his tone, matter-of-fact.

Mother Alder's face went pale and the hairs on the back of her neck stood up as she stared at him, waiting for him to continue, but he did not. "Did you find them? Just tell me."

"They're dead," said Rom.

Mother Alder's brow furrowed, her face twisted. She looked as if someone had driven a stake through her heart. "Tell me," she whispered.

"I found the ship," said Rom.

He spoke each word even slower and more measured than was his normal manner. "Nothing left but a burned-out husk. Barely recognizable, but it was ours."

"Where?" said Mother Alder.

"The Dead Fens," said Rom. "Your vision was correct; that's where they were. The ship lay empty, but we searched. We found a stone keep far back in the deeps. The place was burned, just as the ship. A ruin. Bodies heaped outside. All burned."

"But did you find them?" said Mother Alder.

"Nothing left but bones and ash," said Rom. He turned his face toward her and stared into her eyes. "I saw enough to know that they're dead. I'll chase their ghosts no longer."

"Who did this?" said Mother Alder as tears streamed down her cheeks and bile rose in her throat. "Did you find them? Did you kill them?"

Rom took a deep breath before responding. He filled his tumbler to the brim, then stood, and threw the brandy bottle into the fireplace. It shattered and for a moment the flames burst higher. "The Eotrus and the Malvegils," he said.

"What?" said Mother Alder, shock on her face.

"The two patriarchs themselves were amongst the killers."

"How can that be?" said Mother Alder. "Why would they attack us?"

"Word is, they were hunting pirates. That's their cover story. A grand expedition down from the north. Aradon Eotrus brought a whole troop of men with him."

"Are they saying that our ship was a pirate vessel?" said Mother Alder. "Or that they mistook it for one? That makes no sense."

"Our ship was a target of opportunity. Three other large ships went missing too, and who

262

knows how many small ones. The Eotrus and the Malvegils killed them all. Everyone aboard."

"But why attack Lomerian vessels?" said Mother Alder. "Why kill innocent people?"

"Why do the Northmen do anything?" said Rom.

"Because they are stupid," he said.

"And dangerous.

"And violent.

"Warmongers.

"Killing — that's all they do up there in the mountains. It's a way of life for them. But things have been quiet in the North for a goodly time. Too long it seems. Aradon Eotrus got bored. Got the itch to spill some blood. So he came down south to go hunting."

"Hunting with his new brother-in-law, Torbin Malvegil," said Mother Alder.

"Quite a pair those two make," said Rom. "Barbarians both. Ignorant backwoodsmen unworthy of their titles and stature."

"We'll make them pay, brother," said Mother Alder. "They'll bleed for this."

Rom downed half his cup.

Many minutes went by before he spoke again. "They killed them," he said, his voice beginning to slur.

"My Darilith — my wife. The only woman I've ever loved.

"My little boy.

"They killed him.

"My tiny little baby.

"Murdered. Burned. Nothing left but ash.

"I'm going to take everything from them," said Rom, his eyes watery, his voice, quaking. "Everything they have. Everything that's dear to them. One piece at a time. Even if it takes the rest of my life. I'll have vengeance on the Eotrus. And on the Malvegils. I will see them all dead."

"And I will help you, my brother," said Mother Alder. "We will see this done."

53

DOR MALVEGIL
GUEST QUARTERS

Year 1242, 4th Age
12th Year of King Tenzivel's Rule

Aradon closed and locked the suite's door after the gnome entered. Ob saw the two tumblers laid out on the side table by the fireplace, a fancy bottle of brandy beside them. Two chairs facing each other. Aradon wanted to talk.

"He'll kill me," said Ob as he froze in his tracks.

Aradon shook his head. "You need to tell me what happened up in the turret. Take a seat, sip some brandy, and spew it out. The whole story, top to bottom, nothing left out."

"You don't understand," said Ob. "I'm not saying that he'll be angry. I'm saying that he will actually kill me, dead. Dead. If he ever found out what I saw. What I heard. I'm not saying this lightly or in jest. Are you hearing me?"

"He's a good man," said Aradon.

"Good man or not," said Ob. "Gabe lives by secrets. Before today I knew one of them. The big one. You know of what I speak."

Aradon nodded.

"Now I know more," said Ob. "Too much more. I'm the gnome that knew too much. If you or any

265

of the men ever tell him that I was up there watching — I'm a dead man."

"I don't understand," said Aradon. "What—"

"Neither do I," said Ob. "And I saw it play out. With these ears, I heard every word and whisper. I don't understand some of it, a lot of it, but enough sunk through my thick skull to scare the heck out of me."

"I can see that," said Aradon as he picked up his brandy and took a sip. Ob did the same. They sat. They watched the fire for a goodly while.

"I have to know," said Aradon.

"I know," said Ob.

54

EOTRUS ENCAMPMENT ON THE ROAD NORTH

Year 1242, 4th Age
12th Year of King Tenzivel's Rule

Gabriel stared at baby Claradon as the wet nurse changed the boy. Such a little thing was he. So tiny. So helpless. Not more than three months old, mayhap only two. But so full of life — so expressive, such personality for an infant.

Gabriel had made his decision. One of the hardest of his life. He felt sick over it: his mouth dry, a lump in his throat, his stomach in knots.

He'd done terrible things before, back in olden days. Never by his choice though. Not once. Always on orders from Azathoth.

When he did those deeds, he didn't consider them terrible. They were the will of the one true god — the god of life, love, peace, and all that was good and holy in the world.

Carrying out his will couldn't be bad. Couldn't be evil.

Except that it was.

Or so Gabriel came to believe.

Could he not do a terrible thing again? Just once? For the good of all Midgaard?

The very thought of it made him angry.

What a disgrace. What an insult to himself and to everything he stood for. But his decision was made. It had to be done. The risk was too great.

How ridiculous; the very notion of feeling guilty about the matter, after all he'd seen, all he'd done, all that he was.

Sentimentality; sometimes his bane, but it kept him grounded.

It kept him human.

He couldn't toss it aside; he wouldn't. To do so went against his very nature, for he valued people — always had. Not just the important ones, but all folk of goodly nature, no matter how small, or how ephemeral their lives. A man of conscience; a man of values he would remain until the end of his days.

If that was weakness, so be it.

If that got him killed some day, so be it. He would live and die as the man he always was. A master of his own fate, save for adherence to duty and oaths sworn in times past.

That all said, sometimes, the greater good had to prevail. Sometimes the good of the many outweighed that of the individual. He knew what he had to do. It didn't matter if it was hard, and it didn't matter how it made him feel. He had only to decide when and how to carry it out. That was a challenge in itself, for he must not jeopardize his standing with the Eotrus.

As he sat there, the variables churning in his head for the hundredth time, he felt a gentle, fleeting touch on his shoulder and heard a haunting, melodic voice. "No good can come of an evil deed," said the female voice from just over his shoulder.

Startled, Gabriel turned, but no one was behind him. And no one should be. Only he, the baby, and the wet nurse were in the tent, and the tent flap was secured. Had he been so lost in his thoughts that he didn't hear someone enter?

On his feet in an instant, he turned about, looking for the woman. No one was there. The tent flap still secure. It made no sense, for he was certain the voice came from within the tent. But who was she? And where did she go? Save for the wet nurse, no women traveled north with them toward Dor Eotrus, and it was not the nurse that spoke.

"Who is there?" he said, his voice commanding. "Who spoke? Show yourself."

No reply.

The wet nurse didn't turn around; paid him no heed at all. Then he realized she wasn't moving — still and rigid as a statue did she sit. The child seemed fine, moving his arms and cooing. But the nurse was frozen in place. For a moment he thought her dead, but her eyes were open, her skin warm. But her limbs were locked in place, paralyzed head to toe.

Sorcery.

55

EOTRUS ENCAMPMENT ON THE ROAD NORTH

Year 1242, 4th Age
12th Year of King Tenzivel's Rule

The mystic arts were at work in that tent. That much was clear to Gabriel. But how it crept up on him unnoticed, he could not fathom. His hand immediately went to his ankh, to check it. It was there, as always, hanging securely from its chain about his neck. But it was quiet. It was still.

Gabriel's sword was in his hand, his posture defensive. He stood close over the child. All his instincts to protect it, despite his prior thoughts. He knew the wizard must be close, maybe right beside him, invisible to his eyes.

But he had other senses. He reached out with them. Still he saw nothing, heard nothing out of place.

But then his nose caught a scent.

Flowers and fresh tilled soil.

Faint, but it was there. His ankh remained silent on its chain, of no use at all.

He turned about. And there she was, sitting but inches from him, lovingly caressing the baby's head. Clad in a green and yellow dress was she, her skin green as springtime; her straight hair, long down her back; her eyes a bright blue; her face breathtaking; her body, nothing but perfect curves.

One look, and he knew that he knew her. That he'd seen her before. More than once. Mayhap, many times.

But he had no specific memories of her. None at all. More sorcery at work. He put his hand to his ankh. Cold and silent it remained. Somehow its protections had failed him.

"Hello, dear Gabriel," said the woman, a smile on her face. "Do you remember me?"

Now he did. Memories flooded his mind. "Midgaard," he said. That was what he called her. "The Woman in the Wind."

She smiled again and looked at the baby. "I've been called both, and many other names, some not so kind."

"You stand yet again on knife's edge, Gabriel Garn, the fate of the world in the balance."

"Explain," said Gabriel, his mind racing. He tried to lock that moment into his mind's eye so that he would not forget it, not succumb to her sorcery. His hand gripped the ankh so tightly that had it been of common make, it would have crushed or shattered. He willed the ankh to life, to do its job, and offer its protections. But the fickle thing remained asleep. A useless hunk of stone and metal.

"Be at ease in my presence," said Midgaard. "We are old friends, are we not?" Her piercing gaze bore through him as she studied his reaction.

271

"You would know better than I," said Gabriel. "Names aside, who are you? What sorcery have you hung over me? And why are you here?"

"Always the same questions. And here are my answers. There are those who must not know of me. By suppressing your memories of our meetings, I keep you safe, and I keep my actions secret from those that oppose my goals."

Gabriel opened his mouth to speak, but she put up her hand to stay him. "Now you'll ask my goals and my opponents. I will not answer, save to say, that you and I seek the same ends. We both defend this world with all the skills and knowledge at our command."

"As for why I'm here, I know your mind," she said. "I know your thoughts. Your desires," she said with a coy smile.

"Life or death for this little one is what troubles you. Choose life, and risk all. If he carries the contagion, it will spread. Try as you might, you may not be able to contain it. If it runs free, it will consume the world."

"Does he carry it?"

"Some things even I do not know."

"Do you know, or not?" said Gabriel. "There can be no word games with this. No riddles. Speak plainly."

She shook her head. "So rigid you are when under stress," she said. "So like Thetan are you, yet so different."

"Does he still live? Thetan?"

"You will see him again."

"Do you know if the child has the illness or not?" said Gabriel.

272

"If I did, I would tell you."

Gabriel nodded, satisfied with that answer.

"If the child is free of the contagion," said Midgaard, "Aradon Eotrus will name him his natural born son and raise him as his own. He will remain wedded to Eleanor, even if she bears him no other child."

"If that comes to pass," she said, "the line of kings will be broken."

"The line must not be broken," she said. "The bloodline of Odin must endure."

"And if Azrael was right?" said Gabriel. "About the boy being cured?"

"Then the boy may be the key to the long-sought cure," she said. "The hope of all the world."

"But if you choose death," she said as she stood, her movements lithe, fluid, "then you will lose yourself. You will become what you once rebelled against — a killer of children. Can you bear that?"

"It would give the line of kings a chance," said Gabriel. "Aradon would take another wife. The line might continue through that new union."

"Or it might not," said Midgaard. "The next union as barren as the last. But indeed, the line must continue. But should it, if only by evil deeds? Only by murdering an innocent?"

"You frame the choices, but tell me nothing new," said Gabriel, "for I've thought through all this and more."

"Have you? Think you a hero to sacrifice yourself, your honor, your values, to preserve the bloodline? At what cost? If the child has the cure,

273

he represents the one chance of ending the plague. Without him, the cure may never be found. How could it — when no one else is even looking? No one else even knows to look. And the stain on this world will remain, forever."

"The bloodline is real," said Gabriel. "The cure may not be."

"Azathoth commanded you to black deeds. He told you it was all part of his grand plan, all for the greater good. That the ends justified the means. You sacrificed all to rebel against that notion. Were you wrong?"

"No."

"But you have doubts."

"The plague was a heavy price to pay to free us of Azathoth's yoke. There would have been less suffering in the world had we not stood against him."

"Less freedom," said Midgaard. "Man was not meant to be bound and shackled. It is against your nature."

"What would you have me do?" said Gabriel.

She smiled. "Now we come to it at last."

"I would have you follow your heart," she said. "Do what you know to be good and right, just as you've always done throughout the ages. For as I said, no good can come from black deeds."

"I am not your puppet," said Gabriel. "Pull not my strings."

"You are a hero. Be true to your nature."

"And if the world suffers for it?"

"Then so be it," said Midgaard.

"But I will make the choice easier for you," she said. In her hand appeared a white flower in bloom — a beautiful, delicate thing. "From the great tree of life this comes. From Yddrasil." She placed it in the hand of the child and curled his tiny fingers about it.

"To what end?" said Gabriel.

"The bloom of Yddrasil suffers nothing of death," said Midgaard. "If death be in him, the flower will whither and die before our eyes. If the bloom remains, he carries neither the contagion, nor the plague. And if that is so, that will make him the most important person in all the world."

After a few moments she stood. "We have our answer."

56

THE AZURE SEA, ISLE OF EVERMERE, *EVERMERE BAY*

Year 1267, 4th Age
37th Year of King Tenzivel's Rule

Battle is always chaos. That's its nature. But that fight in Evermere Bay was a special kind of madness. Lord Angle Theta and the heroic men with him, jammed tightly into a single longboat, and fled a horde of bloodthirsty supernatural cannibals, intent on killing them.

Wild was that battle. Loud. No room to move, to maneuver. No sure footing. No help to be had. No chance of escape. The Lomerians had weathered wave after wave of attacks as they fled the bay. But now they were surrounded by the bloodsuckers. The Evermerians massing about them for one final all-out assault.

Angle Theta stood at the far end of the longboat and shouted to catch the attention of his comrades. His blue armor and midnight blue cape covered in blood and gore, his features strong, chiseled in stone, shield in one hand, battle hammer in the other.

Ob was there. So was Artol, Dolan Silk, Glimador Malvegil, Captain Slaayde, Little Tug, and the rest. All of them were battered and bruised, near the end of their strength. But they were ready. Ready to fight.

Theta's voice boomed like thunder. "Don't let them take you," he said. "Fight them to the end, to your last breath, to your last drop of blood. Fight them for Midgaard. For Lomion. For your families. Fight them for Odin and all that's holy. We must stop Korrgonn — the fate of all Midgaard hangs in the balance. To do that, we must escape from here. We must!"

"How the heck are we supposed to do that?" said Captain Slaayde as he looked at the throng of Evermerian boats that surrounded them, closing in."

"By killing them all!" shouted Theta. "And we will! I am with you."

"Fight! Fight! Fight!"

The Evermerians leaped toward the longboat from all directions. Their snarling and howling was so loud that it drowned out all else.

An overhand chop from Theta's hammer crushed the head of the first Evermerian that made the leap. Other blows killed the second, then the third, and the fourth. His shield battered more of them back into the water, breaking bones as it went. A hammer swing sent one Evermerian flying backward twenty feet through the air, to crash into others on a nearby boat, his chest caved in.

Each of the Lomerians fought like mad. They battered back the first wave of leapers. Pummeled them. Crushed them. Stabbed them. The longboat rocked. Little Tug's hammer, Old

Fogey, swept back and forth, bashing, crushing, killing. Artol's hammer did the same.

Glimador threw magic: bolts and blasts and bunk that Ob had no idea the boy had in him – his mother's doing, and good for it.

Ob pushed over an Evermerian that planted her foot atop the gunwale. As she fell back, Glimador took off her head with his sword.

Ob didn't like fighting women. Against his nature it was. To do it, he had to objectify her, to think of her as a monster, which is what she was after all. It still didn't feel right. Ob pushed the thoughts out of his head. That kind of thinking in battle got you killed.

Ob couldn't see farther down the boat; he didn't know what else went on, except for a lot more fighting. He figured Theta was killing them blood suckers but good.

A pause of but a few seconds and another wave came on. More of them that time.

That time, some of them got aboard. The longboat rocked. It twisted. More than once it threatened to capsize.

And then the Duchess was there. She joined the assault. Her pain and anger over her injuries compelled her forth, no longer content to let her subjects do the fighting, the killing. She wanted her revenge. And she was determined to have it by her own hand. She brought her big canoe in fast and rammed it into the Lomerians' longboat, near where Theta stood. The longboat rocked and spun again, but its greater mass and wide width kept it from overturning.

The Duchess retained not even a shadow of her former beauty — her outward appearance now as ugly and foul as her black soul and her stony heart. Her pallor was grayish white with a look more akin to a corpse or a ghoul than a living woman. One hand chopped off, now nothing but a bloody stump halfway to her elbow. One of her eyes was missing — the socket, an ugly, bloody ruin; the other eye, black as pitch, no white to be found. Her cheek torn apart by Dolan's arrow, her teeth and gums ragged and broken, exposed through the bloody hole. Fangs six inches long hung down from her upper jaw; claws even longer rested on the ends of her fingers. Her dress in tatters, covered in blood and soot, her flaming red hair and brows, singed and smoking.

Her claws raked across Theta's shield again and again with a skirling sound and startling speed as sparks went flying. Theta dropped his hammer and pulled his sword. All the while, the Duchess roared curses at him, and spat, foaming at the mouth like a wild beast.

Theta bashed his shield toward the Duchess's face, knocking back her protective hand. The second bash, its strength impossible, broke her arm, snapped her claws. The third bash, not half a moment later, crushed the front of her face. Her fangs shattered, her nose crushed, her jaw twisted at an angle. Theta's kick to her abdomen brought her to her knees. He grabbed a handful of her long hair as she looked up, helpless, broken, finished.

"Mercy," she mumbled through her broken mouth, blood spilling over her lips.

Theta did not pause to consider; he did not hesitate one fraction of a moment. His falchion took off her head in a single blow.

Theta lifted the Duchess's severed head on high for all to see. And his voice boomed across the water. "Your Duchess is dead! Your Duchess is dead! Flee now or share her fate!"

An arrow bounced off Theta's shoulder plate.

That was their answer.

Two, three, four more arrows, pinged against his breastplate, though they failed even to leave the slightest dent.

On came the Evermerians, screaming and cursing as they leapt at the longboat, undeterred, still thousands strong. Like rabid dogs, only death would stop them.

Theta's bag of tricks, now stood barren and empty. "Come forth, and meet your doom," he shouted.

57

THE AZURE SEA, ISLE OF EVERMERE, *EVERMERE BAY*

Year 1267, 4th Age
37th Year of King Tenzivel's Rule

Ob held the gunwale with one hand and worked his axe with the other. An Evermerian landed next to him and half atop Par Tanch who still lay unconscious. Fell right on its back it did, that stinking bloodsucker, head laid open by some blow; all dazed and bleeding. Ob went straight to work on him. A hand axe was a darn good weapon for close quarters.

Somewhere around the fifth or sixth blow that the gnome put into its head, something grabbed Ob by the collar, and lifted him on high.

Teeth bit down on Ob's torso, just below the ribs — that bite, stronger than a war dog's best. He felt no crushing of bone or tearing of flesh so he knew that his mail held, at least for the moment. He swung the axe blindly, but the thing caught his hand. Even as it did, Ob's other hand pulled a dagger and went for where he thought the thing's neck was. He felt the blade sink deep into flesh. The teeth released his side and Ob thrust the dagger in again, still blindly.

Ob twisted and tried to pull free, but the Evermerian held him in an iron grip. Then Ob saw Old Fogey arcing towards him. The hammer caught the Evermerian in the lower abdomen. How the blow completely missed Ob, he never knew. The gnome felt himself flying through the air, pulled along with the Evermerian who wouldn't loose its grip. It seemed like he was thrown twenty feet or more from the longboat, but dear gods, it could not have been that far, could it?

The water was freezing. It hit him like a hammer. Clawed hands grasped at him. He heard shouts of "get him", "get the imp".

His axe was gone. His dagger too. He had only one course of action left to him.

He dove down.

Down into the water's depths with as big a breath of air in his lungs as he could muster. And then he swam — directly away from the longboat, as fast as he could manage. Most folks don't know it, but gnomes are skilled swimmers. Can hold their breaths twice as long or more than a Volsung and they can swim swift like a fish.

He prayed to the gods that no Evermerian went into the water after him. Then he remembered the vast group of blood suckers that swam after their boat, all the way from shore. The speed they had. The endurance. The resistance to the cold. He couldn't face them in the water and live. Not even one of them. He had to get out of there. He turned seaward, away from land, away from their swimmers. He swam and swam until his lungs ached. He went well beyond the

Evermerian boats, but was he out far enough? Was he out of their sights?

He looked up at the water's surface and started up. He was some eight or ten feet down, but he needed air. He had reached his limit. He had to chance surfacing, or else drown.

Still under water, he saw the light — a huge bright flash in the shape of a sphere. It arced through the sky, across his field of vision, high above the water. It came from somewhere beyond the bay, out to sea. It sped toward the longboat, whence Ob came, roaring and sparking, flames burning bright.

Then it was gone.

A moment later, just before Ob broke the surface, he heard the explosion. A mighty blast that roiled the water. Flames lit up the sky.

Ob gasped for air and fought to keep his head above the chop. There was so much screaming. And crackling flames from fire in the water. Many Evermerian boats burned.

Then Ob heard a roar coming at him. Another spherical ball of fire passed over his head, flaming and roaring as it went. It looked like one of the big balls of shot and pitch what Slaayde kept on The Black Falcon. But it couldn't be that, for The Falcon was no more. Destroyed with all hands by a giant sea beast out of Helheim. With his own eyes, Ob saw it happen.

Kaboom went the second blast.

Ob looked for Theta's longboat. Tried to find it through the smoke and the flames. He thought he saw it amid a mass of Evermerian boats not too far off.

It looked intact.

A tall figure stood in it, weapons swinging, tossing bodies this way and that. Was it Theta, Artol, or Tug? He couldn't tell. Then he heard something and spun in the water, turning toward the direction from whence the fiery shots came.

A ship. A big one. Bearing down on him from seaward. As big as The Falcon it was. At that moment, it launched another blast from its forward catapult. A moment later, came a blast from a rear catapult. And with the flashes of light that those shots provided, Ob had a better look at the ship.

His eyes played tricks, cruel tricks indeed, for Ob imagined that it was no random ship of rescue, but that it was The Falcon herself, lately sunk to the bottom of that very bay.

A ghost ship.

A spectre of the past.

And that wasn't all. For Ob imagined then that he saw Claradon Eotrus standing at the prow, his face white as a sheet, directing the catapult shot, the knights of the Dor hovering around him, armor glinting.

A ship of the dead come to save him. To save him from the ravenous dead.

Madness.

More   faerie   stories   come   to   life.

END

GLOSSARY

PLACES

The Realms
Asgard: legendary home of the gods
—**Bifrost**: mystical bridge between Asgard and Midgaard
—**Valhalla**: a realm of the gods where great warriors go after death
Helheim: one of the nine worlds; the realm of the dead
Midgaard: the world of man
—**Lomion**: a great kingdom of Midgaard
Nether Realms: realms of demons and devils
Nine Worlds, The: the nine worlds of creation
Nifleheim: the realm of the Lords of Nifleheim / Chaos Lords
Vaeden: paradise, lost
Yggdrasill: sacred tree that supports and/or connects   the   Nine   Worlds

Places Within The Kingdom Of Lomion
Dallassian Hills: large area of rocky hills; home to a large enclave of dwarves
Dor Caladrill:
Dor Eotrus: see Eotrus Demesne below
Dor Linden: fortress and lands ruled by House Mirtise, in the Linden Forest, southeast of Lomion City
Dor Lomion: fortress within Lomion City ruled by House Harringgold
Dor Malvegil: fortress and lands ruled by House Malvegil, southeast of Lomion City on the west bank of the Grand Hudsar River

286

Dor Valadon: fortress outside the City of Dover
Doriath Forest: woodland north of Lomion City
Dover, City of: large city situated at Lomion's southeastern border
Dyvers, City of: Lomerian city known for its quality metalworking
Farthing Heights: town ruled by House Farthing.
Grommel: a town known for southern gnomes
Hollow, The: a town;
— **Ancestor Hill:** cemetary
— **Azrael's Manor, known as Virent Hall**
— **The Constabulary:** sheriff's office
— **House Falstad Manor**
— **The Odinhome**
Kern, City of: Lomerian city to the northeast of Lomion City.
Kronar Mountains: a vast mountain range that marks the northern border of the Kingdom of **Lomion**
Lindenwood: a forest to the south of Lomion City, within which live the Lindonaire Elves
Lomion City: see below
Portland Vale: a town known for southern gnomes that are particularly skilled bridge building masons
Tarrows Hold: known for dwarves

Parts Foreign
Azure Sea: vast ocean to the south of the Lomerian continent
Darendor: dwarven realm of Clan Darendon

Dead Fens, The: mix of fen, bog, and swampland on the east bank of the Hudsar River, south of Dor Malvegil

Evermere, The Isle of: an island in the Azure Sea, far to the south of the Lomerian continent.

— **The Dancing Turtle**: Evermere's finest inn

Grand Hudsar River: south of Lomion City, it marks the eastern border of the kingdom

Emerald River: large river that branches off from the Hudsar at Dover

Jutenheim: island far to the south of the Lomerian continent (see below for more details).

Karthune Gorge: site of a famed battle involving the Eotrus

Kronar Mountains: foreboding mountain range that marks the northern border of the Kingdom of Lomion.

R'lyeh: a bastion for evil creatures; Sir Gabriel and Theta fought a great battle there in times past.

Thoonbarrow: capital city of the Svarts

Trachen Marches: Theta and Dolan fought the Vhen there.

Tragoss Mor: large city far to the south of Lomion, at the mouth of the Hudsar River where it meets the Azure Sea. Ruled by Thothian Monks.

PEOPLE

Peoples of Midgaard
Emerald elves
Lindonaire elves (from Linden Forest)
Doriath elves (`dor-i`-ath') (from Doriath Forest)
Dallassian dwarves (doll-ass`-ian) (from the Dallassian Hills). Typically four feet tall, plus or minus one foot.
Gnomes (northern and southern), typically three feet tall, plus or minus one foot.
Humans/Men: generic term for people. (In usage, usually includes gnomes, dwarves, and elves)
Lugron (usually pronounced `lou-gron'; sometimes, `lug`-ron'): a barbaric people from the northern mountains, on average, shorter and stockier than Volsungs, and with higher voices.
Picts: a barbarian people
Stowron (usually pronounced `stow`-ron'): pale, stooped people of feeble vision who've dwell in lightless caverns beneath the Kronar Mountains
Svarts (black elves), gray skin, large eyes, spindly limbs, three feet tall or so.
Vanyar Elves: legendary elven people
Vhen, The: cousins of the Lugron; dwell in northernmost mountains; sometimes eat people.
Volsungs: a generic term for the primary people/tribes populating the Kingdom of Lomion

House Alder (Pronounced All-der)
A leading, noble family of Lomion City. Their principal manor house is within the city's borders
Barusa Alder, Lord: Chancellor of Lomion, eldest son of Mother Alder.
Mother Alder: matriarch of the House; an Archseer of the Orchallian Order
Rom Alder: brother of Mother Alder

House Eotrus (pronounced Eee-oh-tro`-sss)
The Eotrus rule the fortress of Dor Eotrus, the Outer Dor (a town outside the fortress walls) and the surrounding lands for many leagues.
Aradon Eotrus, Lord: Patriarch of the House (presumed dead)
Claradon Eotrus, Brother: (Clara-don) eldest son of Aradon, Caradonian Knight; Patriarch of the House; Lord of Dor Eotrus
Donnelin, Brother: House Cleric for the Eotrus (presumed dead)
Ector Eotrus, Sir: Third son of Aradon
Eleanor Malvegil Eotrus: (deceased) Wife of Aradon Eotrus; sister of Torbin Malvegil.
Gabriel Garn, Sir: House Weapons Master (presumed dead, body possessed by Korrgonn)
Jude Eotrus, Sir: Second son of Aradon (prisoner of the Shadow League)
Pontly, Castellan: House Castellan prior to Ob.
Knights & Soldiers of the House:
— **Sergeant Artol**: 7 foot tall veteran warrior.
— **Sir Paldor Cragsmere**: a young knight; formerly, Sir Gabriel's squire
— **Sir Glimador Malvegil**: son of Lord Torbin Malvegil; can throw spells

— **Sir Indigo Eldswroth**: handsome, heavily muscled, and exceptionally tall knight
— **Sir Kelbor**
— **Sir Ganton**: called "the bull" or "bull"
— **Sir Trelman**
— **Sir Marzdan** (captain of the gate, deceased)
— **Sir Sarbek du Martegran** (acting Castellan of Dor Eotrus), a knight captain of the Odion Knights
Malcolm Eotrus: Fourth son of Aradon
Nardon, Eotrus, Lord: Aradon's father
Ob A. Faz III: (Ahb A. Fahzz) Castellan and Master Scout of Dor Eotrus; a gnome
Pellan, Captain (aka, the beardless dwarf)
Stern of Doriath: Master Ranger for the Eotrus (presumed dead)
Talbon of Montrose, Par: Former House Wizard for the Eotrus (presumed dead), son of Grandmaster (Par) Mardack
Tanch Trinagal, Par: (Trin-ah-ghaal) of the Blue Tower; Son of Sinch; House Wizard for the Eotrus. Aliases: Par Sinch; Par Sinch Malaban.
Sverdes, Leren: House physician and alchemist

House Malvegil
Words: *"Honor and vigilance always"*
Torbin Malvegil, Lord: Patriarch of the House; Lord of Dor Malvegil, Lord of the Eastern Marches.
Landolyn, Lady: of House Adonael; Torbin's consort. Of part elven blood.
Clan MacRondal: ruled the Eastern Marches prior to the Malvegils. MacRondal warcry: *"You've no idea what we're made of"*
Eleanor Malvegil Eotrus: (deceased) Wife of Aradon Eotrus; sister of Torbin Malvegil.

Gedrun, Captain: a knight commander in service to Lord Malvegil

Glimador Malvegil, Sir: son of Torbin and Landolyn; working in the service of House Eotrus.

Gorlick the Bold, Master: House Weapons Master – 29th Weapons Master to the Malvegils; son of Thraydin and Bernda

Gravemare, Hubert: Castellan of Dor Malvegil

Hogart: harbormaster of Dor Malvegil's port.

Karktan of Rivenwood, Master: Weapons Master for the Malvegils

Leren Tage: House Physician, circa 1242.

Mordel: Castellan of Dor Malvegil circa year 1,212 - 1,24x.

Ronald, Brother: House Cleric

Rorbit, Par: House Wizard to the Malvegils

Stoub of Rivenwood: Lord Malvegil's chief bodyguard; brother of Karktan (deceased)

Tage, Leren: House physician

Torgrist, Brother: Dor Malvegil's high cleric.

Troopers Bern, Brant, Conger: Malvegillian soldiers

Tybor, Red: House Master Scout; a Pict

Great Beasts, Monsters, Creatures, Animals

Blood Lord: legendary fiends that drink blood and eat humans.

Duergar: mythical undead creatures

Draugar: undead creatures that feast on the living

Dwellers of the Deep: worshippers of Dagon; huge, bipedal fishlike creatures

Fire Wyrm or "**Wyrms**": dragons

Giant (aka Jotun, pl. Jotnar):

292

Jotnar: giants (plural of Jotun)
Jotun: a giant
Ogres:
Leviathan: a huge sea creature
Saber-cat: saber toothed tiger
Shamblers: the walking dead
Trolls, Mountain: mythical creatures of the high mountains
Wendigo: monster of legend that eats people.

The Dead Fens Expedition (Year 1242 of the 4th Age of Midgaard)
The Bellowing Banshee: one of three ships that went missing; its disappearance precipitated the expedition.

The Malvegils:
1. Lord Torbin Malvegil: the Great Lord of the Malvegils
2. McDuff the Mighty: friend of Torbin; a dwarf
3. Master Gorlick the Bold: House Weapons Master
4. Par Rorbit: House Wizard
5. Red Tybor: Master Scout
6. Karktan of Rivenwood: Gorlick's Lieutenant

The Eotrus
1. Lord Aradon Eotrus: the Great Lord of the Eotrus
2. Ob: Master Scout
3. Sir Gabriel Garn: House Weapons Master
4. Par Talbon of Montrose: House Wizard
5. Brother Donnelin: House Cleric
6. Artol: a young warrior of the House

Bonebreakers, The
Famed Lugron mercenary company
Brontack: former leader of the Bonebreakers (deceased)
Gorgorath the Bonebreaker: Captain of the Bonebreakers
Grontor: son of Gorgorath
Hartick: former leader of the Bonebreakers (deceased)
Mog, Old: the Bonebreaker's battle mage
Mordo: 500 lb Lugron soldier
Morgorlain: a Vhen; chieftain of the Stikdar Vhen, son of Gartak, slayer of Domis Darackti, and Lord of the Torg Peaks.
Mort of Bemil's Vane: founder of the Bonebreakers (deceased)
Radsol: a Lugron soldier
Teek: a Lugron soldier
Trench, Old: the Bonebreaker's cook
Tribek: a Lugron soldier
Wolfrick: the leader of rival Lugron mercenary company

Militant and Mystic Orders
Churchmen: a generic term for the diverse group of priests and knights of various orders.
Freedom Guardsmen: soldiery of Tragoss Mor
Grontor's Bonebreakers: a mercenary company. The Lugron, Teek and Tribik belonged to it.
Myrdonians: Royal Lomerian Knights
Orchallian Order, The: an Order of Seers; Mother Alder is one of them.

Order of the Arcane: the wizard members of the Tower of the Arcane

The Evermerians
Ebert Cook: (deceased)
Duchess Morgovia of House Falstad: ruler of Evermere
Moby and Toby: brothers; the "beloveds" of Penny. (deceased)
Penny: a tiny wisp of a girl (deceased)
Rasker: he guards the Duchess's warehouse (deceased)
Rendon, Lord: a noble of Evermere
Slint: aka the "scarecrow"; the Duchess's henchman (deceased)
Trern: he guards the Duchess's warehouse (deceased)

People of The Hollow

Azrael: alchemist/tinker/wizard/Eternal
Bron Mason: a member of the hunters**Brother Jarkin**: town cleric for The Hollow
Constable, The: chief lawman of The Hollow; the marshals report to him.
Ebert Cook: a cook
Falstad, Lady Dahlia: sister of Cassandra Farthing
Duke Baltan of Farthing Heights (deceased); late husband of Lady Cassandra
Farthing, Lady (Duchess) Cassandra Falstad
Farthing, Miss Pennebray: daughter of Lady Cassandra
Hunters, the: men organized by Azrael.

Jaros Tull: famed mercenary captain; one of Azrael's hunters.

Marple Butler: Azrael's butler / lead servant

Mashals, The: lawmen of The Hollow

Mayor Barnton: mayor of The Hollow

Mikel Potter: a skilled potter.

Pennebray (aka Penny): daughter of Lady Cassandra

Refisal: Azrael's elderly gnome assistant

Rintle Blacksmith: a member of the hunters; brother of Triber

Rit Bowman: a member of the hunters

Triber Blacksmith: a member of the hunters; brother of Rintle

Widow Lothborg: enemy of Lady Cassandra Farthing

Others of Note

Azathoth: god worshipped by the Lords of Nifleheim and The Shadow League/The League of Light; his followers call him the "one true god".

Azura du Marnian, the Seer: Seer based in Tragoss Mor. Now travels with the Alders on *The Gray Talon*.

Balthazar: battled with Azrael the Wise in ancient times

Dark Sendarth: famed assassin in league with House Harringgold and House Tenzivel

Harbinger of Doom, The: legendary, perhaps mythical, being that led a rebellion against Azathoth

Jaros, the Blood Lord: foe of Sir Gabriel Garn

McDuff the Mighty: (aka "Red Beard"); a dwarf of many talents

Pipkorn, Grandmaster: (aka Rascatlan) former Grand Master of the Tower of the Arcane. A wizard.

Shadow League, The (aka The League of Shadows; aka The League of Light): alliance of individuals and groups collectively seeking to bring about the return of Azathoth to Midgaard

Talidousen: Former Grand Master of the Tower of the Arcane; created the fabled Rings of the Magi.

Thothian monks: monks that rule Tragoss Mor and worship Thoth

Valkyries: sword maidens of the gods. They choose worthy heroes slain in battle and conduct them to Valhalla.

Titles

Archmage / Archwizard: honorific title for a highly skilled wizard

Archseer: honorific title for a highly skilled seer

Arkon: a leader/general in service to certain gods and religious organizations

Battle Mage: a wizard whose skills are combat oriented.

Castellan: the commander of a fortress/Dor; in service to the Dor Lord.

Constable: chief law enforcement officer of a village or town.

Dor Lord: the leader of a fortress; usually a noble, and often the Patriarch/Matriach of a noble House.

Freesword: an independent soldier or mercenary

Grandmaster: honorific title for a senior wizard of the Tower of the Arcane.

Hedge Wizard: a wizard specializing in potions and herbalism, and/or minor magics.

High Cleric: the senior priest of a church/temple, or of a religious order.

High Magister: a member of Lomion's Tribunal.

High Priest: the senior priest of a church/temple, or of a religious order.

House Cleric: the senior priest in service to a noble House

House Wizard: a senior wizard in service to a noble House

Leren: (pronounced Lee-rhen) generic title for a physician

Mage: a practioner of magic; a wizard.

Magling: a young or inexperienced wizard; also, a derogatory term for a wizard.

Marshal: a law enforcement officer; typically reports to a Constable of village or town.

Master Oracle: a highly skilled seer.

Master Scout: the chief scout/hunter/tracker of a fortress or noble House.

Par: honorific title for a wizard

Seer (sometimes, "Seeress"): women with supernatural powers to see past/present/future events.

Sorcerer: a practitioner of magic; a wizard.

Tower Mage: a wizard that his a member of the Order of the Arcane.

Weapons Master: the senior weapon's instructor/trainer/officer at a fortress.

Wizard: practitioners of magic

THINGS

Miscellany

Alder Stone, The: a Seer Stone held by House Alder

Asgardian Daggers: legendary weapons created in the first age of Midgaard. They can harm creatures of Nifleheim.

Bellowing Banshee, The: one of the ships lost in the Fens

Bloodlust, The: name for the affliction affecting people in The Hollow

Chapterhouse: base/manor/fortress of a knightly order

Dargus Dal: Asgardian dagger, previously Gabriel's, now Theta's

Dor: a generic Lomerian word meaning "fortress"

du Marnian Stone, The: a Seer Stone held by Azura du Marnian

Dyvers Blades: finely crafted steel swords

Ether, The: invisible medium that exists everywhere and within which the weave of magic travels/exists.

Granite Throne, The: the name of the king's throne in Lomion City. To "sit the granite throne" means to be the king.

Mages and Monsters: a popular, tactical war game that uses miniatures

Mithril: precious metal of great strength and relative lightness

Orb of Wisdom: mystical crystal spheres that can be used to open portals between worlds.

Ragnarok: prophesied battle between the Aesir and the Nifleites.

Ranal: a black metal, hard as steel and half as heavy, weapons made of it can affect creatures of chaos

Raspen Brandy:

Rings of the Magi: amplify a wizard's power; twenty created by Talidousen

Seer Stones: magical "crystal balls" that can see far-off events.

Valusian steel: famed for its quality

Weave of Magic; aka the Magical Weave: the source of magic

Yggdrasill: sacred tree that supports and/or connects the Nine Worlds

Languages of Midgaard

Lomerian: the common tongue of Lomion and much of the known world

Magus Mysterious: olden language of sorcery

Militus Mysterious: olden language of sorcery used by certain orders of knights

Old High Lomerian: an olden dialect of Lomerian

Military Units of Lomion

Squad: a unit of soldiers typically composed of 3 to 8 soldiers, but it can be as few as 2 or as many as 15 soldiers.

Squadron: a unit of soldiers typically composed of two to four squads, totaling about 30 soldiers, including officers.

Military Ranks of Lomion

(from junior to senior)

Trooper; Corporal; Sergeant; Lieutenant (a knight is considered equivalent in rank to a Lieutenant); Captain; Knight Captain (for units with Knights); Commander; Knight Commander (for units with Knights); Lord Commander (if a noble); General (for Regiment sized units or larger)

ABOUT GLENN G. THATER

For more than twenty-five years, Glenn G. Thater has written works of fiction and historical fiction that focus on the genres of epic fantasy and sword and sorcery. His published works of fiction include the first ten volumes of the *Harbinger of Doom* saga: *Gateway to Nifleheim*; *The Fallen Angle*; *Knight Eternal*; *Dwellers of the Deep*; *Blood, Fire, and Thorn*; *Gods of the Sword*; *The Shambling Dead*; *Master of the Dead*; *Shadow of Doom*; *Wizard's Toll*; the novella, *The Gateway*; and the novelette, *The Hero and the Fiend*.

Mr. Thater holds a Bachelor of Science degree in Physics with concentrations in Astronomy and Religious Studies, and a Master of Science degree in Civil Engineering, specializing in Structural Engineering. He has undertaken advanced graduate study in Classical Physics, Quantum Mechanics, Statistical Mechanics, and Astrophysics, and is a practicing licensed professional engineer specializing in the multidisciplinary alteration and remediation of buildings, and the forensic investigation of building failures and other disasters.

Mr. Thater has investigated failures and collapses of numerous structures around the United States and internationally. Since 1998, he has been a member of the American Society of Civil Engineers' Forensic Engineering Division (FED), is a Past Chairman of that Division's Executive Committee and FED's Committee on Practices to

Reduce Failures. Mr. Thater is a LEED (Leadership in Energy and Environmental Design) Accredited Professional and has testified as an expert witness in the field of structural engineering before the Supreme Court of the State of New York.

Mr. Thater is an author of numerous scientific papers, magazine articles, engineering textbook chapters, and countless engineering reports. He has lectured across the United States and internationally on such topics as the World Trade Center collapses, bridge collapses, and on the construction and analysis of the dome of the United States Capitol in Washington D.C.

CONNECT WITH GLENN G. THATER ONLINE

Glenn G. Thater's Website:
http://www.glenngthater.com

To be notified about new book releases and any special offers or discounts regarding Glenn's books, please join his mailing list here: http://eepurl.com/vwubH

BOOKS BY GLENN G. THATER

THE HARBINGER OF DOOM SAGA
GATEWAY TO NIFLEHEIM
THE FALLEN ANGLE
KNIGHT ETERNAL
DWELLERS OF THE DEEP
BLOOD, FIRE, AND THORN

GODS OF THE SWORD
THE SHAMBLING DEAD
MASTER OF THE DEAD
SHADOW OF DOOM
WIZARD'S TOLL
VOLUME 11+ *forthcoming*

THE HERO AND THE FIEND
(A novelette set in the Harbinger of Doom universe)

THE GATEWAY
(A novella length version of *Gateway to Nifleheim*)

HARBINGER OF DOOM
(Combines *Gateway to Nifleheim* and *The Fallen Angle* into a single volume)

THE DEMON KING OF BERGHER
(A short story set in the Harbinger of Doom universe)

Visit Glenn G. Thater's website at http://www.glenngthater.com for the most current list of my published books.

www.ingramcontent.com/pod-product-compliance
Lightning Source LLC
Chambersburg PA
CBHW022022240626

47154CB00007B/2226